A KISS BETWEEN FRIENDS

"What are you doing here?" Becca asked.

"I had something important to tell you."

"Okay?"

"I want you."

The beer bottle slipped from her grasp, shattering into a thousand pieces on her porch, but she couldn't pull her gaze from his. "What did you just say?"

Nick smiled at her, the picture of ease. "I said I want you. I wanted you at eight. I wanted you at eighteen. And I want you now. That part has never been in question. Doubt whatever you want, but don't doubt that. I want you. Trip and Alex, the town, they all think you're my match because I can't stop talking about you, can't even look at anyone else. For me, there's only you."

Pushing off the swing and tiptoeing around the broken glass so she could see him better, she asked, "But what about our friendship?"

Nick edged closer to her, one step, but the impact on her heart was the weight of a thousand. It felt like they'd been walking toward each other for a lifetime, only to finally find the right route, the right location, the right way to each other.

Tentatively, he reached for her hand, his gaze trained on their linked fingers as though he were watching something miraculous happening. "I don't know." Then he flicked his eyes up to hers. "But if I don't do this, I'm going to go insane."

And then in one more move, he had her in his arms, his face coming down to meet hers as he captured her lips with his . . .

Books by Melissa West

RACING HEARTS

WILD HEARTS

SILENT HEARTS

Published by Kensington Publishing Corporation

Silent Hearts

Melissa West

LYRICAL SHINE
Kensington Publishing Corp.
www.kensingtonbooks.com

LYRICAL SHINE BOOKS are published by

Kensington Publishing Corp.
119 West 40th Street
New York, NY 10018

All Kensington titles, imprints, and distributed lines are available at special quantity discounts for bulk purchases for sales promotion, premiums, fund-raising, educational, or institutional use.

Special book excerpts or customized printings can also be created to fit specific needs. For details, write or phone the office of the Kensington Sales Manager: Kensington Publishing Corp., 119 West 40th Street, New York, NY 10018. Attn. Sales Department. Phone: 1-800-221-2647.

Lyrical Shine and Lyrical Shine logo are trademarks of Kensington Publishing Corp.

First Electronic Edition: May 2016
eISBN-13: 978-1-61650-829-6
eISBN-10: 1-61650-829-9

First Print Edition: May 2016
ISBN-13: 978-1-61650-830-2
ISBN-10: 1-61650-830-2

Printed in the United States of America

To my amazing readers' group. Thank you for your continued support.

ACKNOWLEDGMENTS

As always, many thanks to God for challenging me to be better and for providing strength.

Thank you to my agent, Nicole Resciniti, for being my rock, for knowing so much more than me, and for keeping me focused.

Thank you to my editor John Scognamiglio, production editor Rebecca Cremonese, marketing staff Michelle Forde, Kimberly Richardson, Lauren Jernigan, and all the amazing staff at Kensington for making this book possible. You are all so wonderful. I truly feel blessed to work with each of you.

I could not write without the love and support of my family—my husband, Jason, my two amazing daughters Rylie and Lainey, and my parents, sister, and extended family. You keep me going.

At this point, I would never complete a book without the kindness, humor, and friendship of Rachel Harris and Cindi Madsen. I am so thankful to call you friends and learn from you both daily.

Thank you to Staci Murden for reading everything I write, for telling me what's crazy, and for always saying it's good . . . even when it isn't yet. You are such a wonderful friend.

And thank you to YOU for reading this book, for checking out my other works, and for being part of the reading community. You are the reason we authors are allowed to do what we love!

Chapter One

"Now, that's a heart attack waiting to happen." Becca Stark eyed the overflowing plate before her, all piled high with eggs and grits and bacon. Dear Lord, bacon. The smell of the guilty meat hit her nostrils, and though she'd given the stuff up thanks to her genetic predisposition to have the cholesterol of a person who ate cheeseburgers with a side of cheeseburgers, her stomach growled.

Why couldn't broccoli *taste* like bacon? Or better, just make bacon healthy. Or simply make a pill that kept your cholesterol in check, and then Becca rolled her eyes at herself. "They have a pill, idiot."

"Who you calling an idiot? And what pill?" Sage Blackson, the cook, called from inside the kitchen of the diner. Like always, a navy bandanna covered his gray head, and Becca knew if the health inspectors allowed it, he'd have a cigarette dangling from his lips, too.

Come to think of it, she should thank those inspectors the next time they were in town, if only for the lawsuit they'd saved the diner, in turn saving Becca's job.

"Nothing," Becca finally replied, her eyes back on the bacon, her stomach continuing its plea. Forget what was healthy or her cholesterol, she was starving!

Taking a peek at Sage through the diner's serve window to make sure the cook wasn't watching, she reached for the extra plate of bacon he'd set to the side for the next round of orders. But before her fingers could lock around a delicious strip, Sage popped her hand and pointed his spatula at her.

"You remember what the doctor said."

Pouting, Becca crossed her arms. "It's not fair; my cholesterol isn't that high. And how do *you* know what *my* doctor said? I haven't eaten yet today, and I took over the morning shift so Caroline could go to her chiropractor."

She scanned the overcrowded diner. The walls were yellow on three sides, red on the fourth. The tables and booths were all red, puffy plastic and metal trim. The floor was black and white alternating tile. Vintage posters hung around the room. It had a fifties vibe without trying too hard—very much like Sage himself. And though he refused to admit that he owned the diner, Becca knew he did.

Everyone in town came there or to Patty's for breakfast, so the place was always packed, the food always delicious—though decidedly fattening—which had added more than a few inches to Becca's waist and thighs over the years.

Still . . . she eyed the bacon again.

"You know he's not going to give you any, so you might as well stop drooling." Willow, the other waitress on duty, settled in beside Becca and leaned against the counter. "That Caroline's got herself in a pickle for sure. You know why she landed at the chiropractor's office, don't you?"

Becca looked around like she'd entered a completely different conversation. Then she remembered this was Triple Run, Kentucky, population 2,587, and home to at least that many conversations, all happening at the same time.

"Um, no, I have no idea why she went to the chiropractor, nor do I care. Nor should you. Or you." Becca pointed at Sage because while Willow was a gossip, she had nothing on Sage.

Sage ignored her. "Don't just stand there, woman, hurry up and tell us."

Becca rolled her eyes, but there was no escaping this now.

Willow leaned in conspiratorially. " 'Cause she threw out her back doing the twisted taco with Mayor Phillips." She covered her mouth as she giggled and glanced around before continuing her story. "Rumor says they started shacking up a month ago. Even did it in the town hall, right in the mayor's office. Said they broke his desk. Twice. And now they've gone and broken Caroline's back."

"Her back's not broken. That's ridiculous," Becca said, which made all the rest of Willow's claims about as thin as paper. But Caroline *had* acted strange lately, and the mayor certainly had been single a long time. Hmm . . .

Then Becca sighed heavily, annoyed at herself for falling prey to Willow and Sage's antics. Again.

"Never would've suspected those two," Sage said, shaking his head. "And he's a widower. She should know better."

"What does his being a widower have to do with anything?" Becca asked, then fisted her hands and cursed herself for fanning the gossip flame. The problem was there wasn't much else to do in Triple Run than gossip.

It was Sage's turn to lean in closer and peer around. "Them widowers are feisty."

"And how exactly would you know that?"

The sixty-two-year-old's eyes fell on Penny Lewis by the door, who was every bit of seventy, and suddenly Becca had lost her appetite. Such a shame, too—no one made bacon like Sage.

"And that's my cue to exit this absurd conversation."

But as Becca carried over table three's order, she found she was no longer jealous of the eggs and bacon and grits they were about to enjoy. No, she was jealous of Caroline, which had to be the most ridiculous thing she'd thought all day. Maybe all week. So what if Caroline had injured herself doing the twisted taco? So what if even Caroline had a better sex life than she did? What did it matter? She had things going on, lots of things, epic, big things.

Only that was a lie.

She had nothing going on; so little, in fact, that her life played out like one of those boring commercials for at-home medication delivery. And then, to add more yuck to her life's blandness, Becca's dating life revolved around the town's belief that she wasn't one of the girls but rather one of the guys. Or, more specifically, one of the Hamiltons. And there was one great problem with that belief—no, two problems.

Problem one: She wasn't a Hamilton.

Problem two, which made problem one super important: She was in love with Nick Hamilton.

See, Becca might have spent her childhood cutting through the woods behind her house, which led to the Hamiltons' farm. She might have helped them toilet paper all of Crestler's Key after they claimed to be the home of horse racing, when everyone knew that title belonged to Triple Run. And she might even have taken their dare to climb to the top of Triple Run Baptist and ring the church bell . . . naked. But none of those things made her a Hamilton.

No, Becca would now, and unless the tides changed, forever be, a Stark—the very opposite of the Hamiltons.

The Hamiltons were royalty in Triple Run. They owned Hamilton Stables, the renowned Thoroughbred breeding and training farm. They had trophies and titles with their name on them. And they weren't just richer than God, they were respectable and civilized.

The Starks had no idea what either word meant.

The Hamilton brothers ruled not only all of horse racing but all of Triple Run. They were kings, and though Becca knew all three of the brothers, and she knew middle brother Nick better than anyone knew him, she would never really exist in their world. And she was fine with that fact. Completely and totally fine. Now if only she could convince her heart of as much.

But then her heart had never been safe where Nick Hamilton was concerned.

Her mind drifted through the years of friendship, always being there for each other—Nick holding her hand when her grandmother died, her comforting him through his mother's death, holding him close as he cried after his fiancée's death. And then Carter Hamilton, his father, had died, and something inside Nick seemed to die along with him. Like maybe he couldn't take anymore.

Becca went back to the counter, grabbed the next order, and continued around the diner, smiling and handing out food until she came to the booth in the back corner, a very pregnant Kate Hamilton working to slid into the booth, though her swollen belly had other ideas.

"Need some help?"

Kate's head lifted, her face flushed, and Becca had to fight off a smile. "Can you get this baby out of me? Because then yes, I'd love some help. Right this second, in fact."

"Aw, honey, I'm sorry, but I'm no help there. When were you due?"

"Eight days ago."

Becca cringed. She knew from her sister that pregnancy was almost never fun, but certainly not in those final weeks and days. To go past your due date had to rank high on the list of living the most miserable existence on the planet.

"I'm sorry. Maybe you should be lying down at home?"

"My mama's there with the kids so I could get out for a bit. I'm supposed to meet Alex here, but they were running a new colt this morning, and Nick and Trip were both there to see how he did."

At the mention of Nick, Becca's gaze snapped up. "Nick? I thought he was still out of town."

Since Carter had passed away and Nick took over Hamilton Industries, he'd been traveling more often than he'd been home, all in an effort to keep up faith in the company and build new connections. And if Becca knew Nick at all, she suspected he hated every minute of it.

The Nick Hamilton Becca knew wasn't a businessman at all. He was an outdoorsman, who used to talk about fishing professionally and sponsorships, but then he went to Northwestern, met his fiancée Britt, she died, and everything changed.

Now Kate's eyes sparkled and she smiled wide. "He just got home today. Want me to text Alex to bring Nick with him?"

Becca jerked back. "What? No. Not at all. Why would I want Nick to come to the diner?" She had taken to smoothing her apron and checking her long brunette ponytail, which did nothing more than make Kate's smile widen

"Whatever you say. But yes, he's home. I imagine he'll call you soon. Don't y'all talk every day or something? He's always saying 'Becca said this' or 'Becca said that.' I bet the man can't make a decision without you."

A smile found its way across Becca's face before she could pocket it, and Kate turned positively giddy. "You know—"

"Hey, babe, sorry I'm late." Alex rushed up to the table, kissed his wife, then pulled back to examine the damage. "Scale of one to ten, how pissed off are you?"

A strange look crossed Kate's face as she stared at her husband, seriously considering the question, and Becca had to laugh at the nervousness on Alex's face. She never would have guessed the wildest Hamilton would now be such a worried husband and father. "At you or God? Because right now it's neck and neck. You know I can't get into these booths without your help or a solid crowbar, and I forgot my crowbar at home."

"I'm sorry." He kissed her again and then whispered something in her ear that had her smiling again. "Does that smile mean I'm forgiven?"

"That smile means you're dirty. But yes, forgiven."

Alex released a breath, then, spying Becca there, walked over. "Sorry, Bec, I didn't see you there. Was too distracted by my imminent death, but looks like I'll survive another day." Becca laughed, and he kissed her cheek before slipping into the booth across from his pregnant wife, who had pushed the table as far away from herself as possible and still had to sit sideways, her feet stretched out across the booth's seat. Kate gained forty-plus pounds with each child, ballooned up like an inflatable, and then shrunk back down immediately after birth, like all the air had been let out of her. It mystified Becca, and she suspected she wouldn't be so lucky in her own pregnancy. If she ever became pregnant, or married, for that matter.

"You talked to Nick yet?"

Becca took out her order pad and shrugged. "No, but I'm sure he's busy."

Alex and Kate both watched her curiously, and Becca wondered if she'd gotten some of the maple syrup from the bottle she took Pastor Wilkins on her hand, then touched her face or hair, and she was now slathered in the stuff.

It wouldn't be the first time that had happened.

"Um . . ." Becca glanced around, unable to handle the scrutiny. "Is there a sign over my head or something? What are y'all staring at?"

Alex opened his mouth to speak, but Kate slapped his hand and his head snapped over to his wife instead. "Hey! I didn't say anything."

"That's right, you didn't. And we need to keep it that way." Kate pointed at her husband, and Becca laughed because pointing and spouting out orders was a Triple Run thing, and to see Kate doing it meant she'd become one of them.

Becca tried to let it go—surely whatever they were talking about was none of her business—but she'd always been more curious than a cat, and that curiosity had stung her more times than she could count. Still . . . "Say anything about what?"

"Nothing," Kate said. "It's a stupid thing." She said this with the sort of laugh that sounded less like a laugh and more like a struggle not to choke.

"All right." Becca felt like she'd entered yet another random Triple Run conversation, but this time something told her the conversation involved her.

"It's just—" Alex started, and Kate slapped his hand again. "Good God, woman, stop it."

"Well, we talked about this."

"And I don't agree with where we left it."

"It's not your decision to make."

"No one else's making a damn decision, so might as well be me."

"Stop it."

Becca was genuinely perplexed now. "Guys, I'd love to stand here and try to work out . . . whatever this is. But I have other tables, so if you could get to the ordering part." She smiled, and Kate smiled, but Alex still looked offended at his wife's antics.

Kate handed over her menu without looking at it, like most everyone else in Triple Run. In a town where everyone was a regular, she could predict orders before they were spoken. "Three pancakes, scrambled eggs, side of bacon and grits. Oh, and toast. And do you have any fresh apple butter or honey?"

Ohhh-kay, Becca thought. So she could normally predict orders, but she never would have expected Kate to order quite that much food. Surely it wouldn't all fit inside her, but then, Becca had never been pregnant before. Maybe the baby inhaled food the way the rest of us inhaled air. A shudder worked through her, the thought scaring her more than it should. She would have to rethink the whole having-a-baby thing—the insane hunger coupled with hulklike mood swings and then the pain of actually delivering made the whole thing seem this side of crazy. But then, Becca didn't even have a husband or boyfriend. The last thing she should be worrying about was a baby.

Focusing back on Kate, she said, "We have both. And homemade cherry jam."

Kate's face lit. "Cherry jam? That sounds amazing."

"It's fantastic on the biscuits."

"Ooo, biscuits. I'll take those, too. With the cherry jam." She placed her hands on her belly, clearly pleased with herself.

The women both looked over at Alex, who appeared both impressed and shocked. "Did you leave anything for the rest of the diner?" But at Kate's glare, he quickly corrected himself. "Um, I meant to say I'll have the same thing." Then he lowered his voice and added to Becca, "And a to-go box or eight."

Becca laughed and went on her way, but once she was a few steps away, she turned back and caught the couple in a deep conversation, Kate lecturing Alex, forever the teacher, and Alex shrugging her off, forever the free spirit. She started to laugh until she heard Kate say, "This is Nick's thing. We can't intervene."

"Then he needs to do something. You know as well as I do that he wants her, that she's his match. He needs to tell Becca."

"Shhh, keep your voice down," Kate said, just as Becca disappeared behind the counter.

Suddenly the diner was too hot, her skin prickly, her heart too heavy in her chest.

So that was what Alex wanted to tell her, what Kate thought Nick himself should confess. It was inevitable, right, but that didn't stop the pain.

Nick had met someone.

Chapter Two

Nick stepped off the elevator and waved hello to Violet, the front desk admin. Fresh coffee hit his nose from the open lounge area beside Violet, and he made a note to come back there after setting down his things.

The office had been renovated in the last two months, and where it used to have a rustic feel, everything was now bright. Bright blue, bright white. Too bright, if you asked Nick, which they hadn't, because they knew what he would say—do whatever you want.

Still, he wished he'd voiced a little opinion on this. For his eyes' sake, if for no other reason.

He continued on toward his office in the back corner, hoping if he kept his head down no one would approach him. His look had manifested over the years from sleek suits to dress shirt/tie/slacks, to it was a miracle if he wore a tie at all now. His hair, which was once cropped short and gelled into place, now flowed freely—all right, recklessly—around his head in what he'd deemed his new style. But really it was more a product of getting out of the shower and heading to the office without worrying about the state of his hair. Or his clothes. Or his beard, apparently, because he hadn't taken the time to shave in three days.

The problem, or at least one of them, was that he dreaded going to the office. Like root canal dread. His father had passed away almost five years ago and yet still every time he walked into a room it was like everyone there expected him to be Carter. Then they would realize it was just Nick—again—and sigh heavily before going back to work.

Which was why Nick had started considering other jobs. He needed to feel like he existed again, like he could breathe. Lord knew he couldn't breathe in that office, with the long looks and sad faces and constant questions about whether he would sell now that his father was gone.

The truth was they'd had offers, but Nick couldn't imagine selling his father's company. It would be like watching Carter die all over again, and Nick had barely survived it the first time.

Now, five years later and he still felt like there was a hole in his chest that refused to heal. The hole began with his mother's death, then Britt's, and then, when his father died, the hole burst wide open, a disaster left behind, and Nick no longer felt like himself. Sure, he talked to his brothers, Alex and Trip, and tried to find commonality there, but he was always far more like his father than his brothers, and now he didn't know how to be at all.

But that was the thing about running a business—he had no choice. All these people were counting on him to stand strong, put aside the ache and emptiness, and continue on. To get past it.

If only he could.

Now, the only person he could stand to be around was his best friend, Becca, though he knew he had to be grating on her, too. Thankfully, she'd yet to say it. Becca had a way of being there without feeling like a burden. They would sit outside and stare at the stars, neither of them talking, yet somehow a conversation flowed between them. Everything made sense around Becca, the complicated became simple, the difficult became easy.

Nick felt so much better around her that when Carter had first died, he'd spent a full week at her house, unable to be in his own, unable to take the memories. And she'd allowed it without hesitation, made up her guest room and let him be.

The idea of living his life without her was unimaginable, though by now he'd learned to keep most people at arm's length. Feelings and trust equaled pain, and though he knew his brothers had opinions about his relationship with Becca, he didn't care.

Despite the fact that he'd been attracted to her from the moment he first laid eyes on her when they were eight years old and that attraction had only blossomed, they were friends, nothing more. And that's how it would always be. Even if the question *what if* swarmed through his mind more often than not when he was around her. Still, it was better this way.

At least that was what he told himself.

He had just reached for his office's door handle when a small voice said, "Nick?"

Closing his eyes, Nick attempted to ignore his assistant, Tracy—not because he was a jerk but because he hadn't had his morning coffee, and he didn't feel he could have a conversation without his tone showing every bit of the aggravation he felt.

Maybe he *was* a jerk.

"I'm sorry, but there's someone here to see you. In the conference room?"

Adjusting his glasses, Nick ran a hand through his hair, then over the three-day-old scruff on his jaw, which was less scruff and more beard by this point.

"Who is it?" His eyes fell on Tracy, her curly hair a mess around her head like always, her brown eyes wide with barely contained fear. Nick sighed.

Was he really that bad? Years ago, Tracy was all smiles and laughs. She'd pop into his office without hesitation, but something had changed, and now she tiptoed around him like he'd blow up at a moment's notice. Which he'd never done—not once. He never yelled at his staff, never raised his voice much at all. But while he could control his voice, he couldn't control his demeanor, and clearly he was scaring his staff by his brooding attitude alone.

"Never mind, I'll go." He opened his door, set his laptop bag in a chair inside, then closed it again without bothering to turn the light on and set off for the conference room at the opposite end of the floor from his office. That gave him a solid fifteen seconds to throw on a half smile and try for pleasantries.

He tried to remind himself that his family had connections all over the world, his father had friends all over the world, and those people deserved his attention and respect, even if he didn't feel like giving it. That was the least he could do for his father's memory.

Drawing a long breath, Nick pushed through the door of the conference room, and immediately a memory of his first time walking into that room hit him. His father had been at the head of the table, the board filling the rest of the chairs, and Carter had glanced over with nothing but pride. That pride had given Nick the courage to go in there and stand tall while Carter announced that he would be stepping down and Nick would be taking over. Talk about large shoes to fill. There was only one Carter Hamilton.

Still, Nick had all the credentials—double bachelors in business and management from Northwestern, an MBA from Harvard. Then he and Britt had spent the better part of a year traveling around the world, him learning everything he could about business along the way. He'd worked odd end jobs before settling back home in Triple Run, and it had taken a surprisingly small amount of time for Carter to ask Nick to take over Hamilton Industries. It was a natural move, and Nick was ready.

He always knew his father was there to answer questions, provide guidance, and they had met every Wednesday for years to go over business. It was a comfortable move, all of management still in place, so Nick's job was less doing anything substantial and more not screwing up what everyone else was doing. In the end, he helped the business continue to grow. He'd bought three smaller companies since he took over and absorbed them within Industries without any problem. Until finally Industries hit a wall, and sales began to slowly but surely decline.

Soon larger businesses or competitors were eager to do to Hamilton Industries what Industries had done to those three other companies. He'd received pitches from various companies on and off for the last year. And as Nick took in the three suits seated in his conference room around the long rectangular table, he knew he was in for yet another pitch.

They stood the moment Nick entered, and immediately he wished he'd kept to asking Tracy who was waiting for him. Then he could have had her show them out, made up some excuse that he had an emergency meeting come up, something. Now there was no getting out of this without being an ass, and while Nick wanted to take on that role, and internally he had, externally he was still the good Hamilton brother, unable to piss anyone off. Forever concerned with family image.

"Gentlemen," Nick said, holding out a hand to each of them. "What can I do for you today?"

"Mr. Hamilton—"

"Nick." There was a lot Nick could take. Coming here unannounced and then standing in his conference room and calling him what would always be Carter's name wasn't one of them. Add to that the casual expression on the man's face and the way he stood there wearing a polo shirt and khakis instead of a suit, and already Nick wasn't a fan of the guy.

"My apologies. Nick, my name is William Compton, and I'm the president of First Star Investing. These are Dean and Wyatt, my sons." Nick eyed the other two men, and it wasn't lost on him why William had brought them. Clearly, they were a family business, just like the Hamiltons, and William was hoping that singular similarity would sway Nick.

He hoped in vain. And though the man seemed like a nice guy, it still rubbed Nick the wrong way that he'd shown up unannounced.

"Okay, I'm assuming you aren't here to talk about diversifying my portfolio, so what can I do for you?"

"We would like to discuss our interest in Hamilton Industries."

Nick remained standing. "I appreciate your time, gentlemen, but we aren't for sale."

The men eyed one another, a quizzical expression on each of their faces. "Um, well, we are prepared to offer you a generous sum for the business," William said, continuing his pitch.

He had balls, Nick could give him that, but the idea of money being of interest to Nick did little more than cause him to laugh.

People came here and assumed that money meant something to him, when nothing could be further from the truth. His employees, his family's legacy, all his father's work over the years, those were the things that mattered to him.

He had enough money to buy a small island. Or maybe a large island. He wasn't sure, but plenty, and the last thing he needed was more money. Between his role in Industries, his share of earnings at Stables, and his inheritance from his father's death, he was a very, very wealthy man.

But through death and death and more death, he'd learned that money couldn't buy you a damn thing. Not really. Not the important stuff. So his money was tied up in different places, earning him still more money. It was such a trivial thing to him that there were moments when he grew frustrated and would log on to some charity, donate ten or twenty thousand dollars, whatever made him feel better in that moment, only to do it all over again a month later.

Money was nothing to Nick. William, however, appeared genuinely offended at Nick's response. "You haven't heard the offer yet."

"I don't need to. There is no amount of money you can offer me to make me consider selling. None."

"But—"

"Look, I have a very busy day ahead of me, and you showed up without calling, which tells me that you neither respect my time nor my wishes for my family's business. Even if I decided to sell, I wouldn't sell to you."

Nick started away when William called out, "But, Mr. Hamilton—Nick—we didn't show up unannounced. Your brothers planned this meeting."

Nick stopped short and pivoted back around. "Excuse me?"

"Trip and Alex scheduled this meeting with us." William's confusion was enough to send Nick over the edge.

Trip. It had to be Trip. His youngest brother Alex would never go behind his back this way without eldest brother Trip leading the way. But reacting in front of the Comptons wouldn't fix the issue between him and his brothers, and besides, he was already dangling so close to crazy that he didn't need to risk losing it.

Instead he swallowed hard and set his jaw. "Well, they were mistaken. I have no interest in selling Hamilton Industries, and as I'm sure you're aware, I'm the president. Not Trip. And not Alex. Me. Now, we're done here."

He stormed out, his head throbbing more and more with each step.

Tracy stood quickly when she saw him. "Are you okay?"

"Get Trip on the phone." And he slammed his office door.

So much for image.

His phone buzzed and Tracy's shaky voice said, "Line one."

"Thank you."

Then Nick hit line one, swiveled in his chair to try to keep the rest of the office from seeing what was happening. He hated this, every bit of it. The animosity between the brothers, the tension whenever they saw one another. When had it gotten this bad? And while Nick wanted to correct it, find a way to talk without yelling, today wasn't going to be the day.

"Nick," Trip said.

"What the hell do you think you're doing?"

"Alex and I agreed that it was time you consider a solid offer. Compton's is a solid offer."

Nick reached for his stress ball, clenching and releasing, clenching and releasing, until finally he clenched so tight the thing burst.

He tossed the ball across the room, where it hit a frame, which then crashed to the floor.

Fantastic.

"It isn't your decision to make," Nick said, once he could trust himself to speak without yelling. "And this is the first and last time you involve yourself with my business. Understand? I'm the one traveling all over, maintaining Industries. I'm the one who has run this thing for the last nine years. Not you. You know nothing about this side of our business. Nothing. And you will have no say in selling it. We have more than a thousand employees across the country. They are scared out of their minds that we're going to sell and they will lose their jobs and I've assured every one of them that it isn't going to happen. Because it isn't. My company, my call."

Nick drew a breath that rattled more than he'd like. He sounded like Carter and he knew it, and he knew Trip would call him out on it.

Instead, Trip sighed into the phone. "Look, we know Dad's death hit you the hardest, that you carried it for a long time."

"You have no idea. You and Alex were able to live that last year in peace, while I had to watch him slowly die, had to plan out every element of his death and burial. You didn't do a damn thing. You had no right to throw this at me. You should have called. Asked. We should have had a conversation about this. Numerous conversations."

"We've had conversations."

"You should have tried again."

"You would have said no."

"Damn straight."

"You are being ridiculous. When are you going to see that?"

"It's my decision."

"It's time," Trip said, softer this time. "The business is declining. It's a great time to sell. And you're . . ."

"I'm what?"

He could hear Trip's hesitation.

"I'm what?"

"You're over it. You've lost whatever it was that drove you to succeed. Now you're a vessel there, you're miserable, and you're making the staff miserable. Look out into the office. Look at the faces of the people working for you. For us. And be honest—do they look happy?"

A chill worked down Nick's spine. "It's expected after a death."

"He didn't just die, Nick. Dad's been dead for five years now, and I know it's hard—"

"You don't!" So much for not yelling.

"I do! And so does Alex. He was our dad, too, and we miss him, too. But we have to move on. We have to continue our lives."

Nick wanted to scream that it was easy for them to move on, to continue their lives. They had lives, had wives and kids and a future. Nick had nobody, and if they took Industries, then he'd lose the last thing he had keeping him from falling apart.

"You can't sell without my signature."

"You're right. But we're hoping eventually you'll see reason. It's time, man. When are you going to see that?"

Never, Nick thought.

"You shouldn't have thrown this at me."

Trip sighed again. "Fine, I'll give you that. We shouldn't have. And I'm sorry. But we're worried about you."

"You don't need to worry about me. I'm fine."

"Are you? Because I don't think you are."

Nick opened his mouth to argue, then closed it and turned around to look out into the office. Sure enough, everyone he could see appeared miserable. Had he really made it this bad here? Clearly so.

"Look, I've gotta go."

"Think about it, okay?"

Nick drew a breath. "Fine."

"Nick . . ."

"I said I would."

They hung up, and Nick wondered how he'd fallen so far without realizing it. How he'd let the business and its people turn into this, this . . . whatever the hell this was. He needed to get out of there, to think, and there was only one place to go.

Becca Stark, you're about to get a visitor. And the way things were headed, he might never leave.

Chapter Three

Becca toweled off her long wet hair, her skin still clammy from the mix of the heat outside, the humidity from her shower, and her desire to keep her A/C turned off. She liked to save on heating and cooling from September through November, but with summer holding on strong, September still felt like July and she was struggling to keep away from the controller, eager to drop that baby down to 65.

All right, 68. She was hot, not crazy.

But with only her income to keep the power on, she had to be responsible. So she sauntered over to her dresser, opened the top drawer, and pulled out a white tank top. Then she moved to the bottom drawer on the right and tugged out a pair of tiny cotton shorts she'd stuffed there the day before.

Once dressed, she let her damp hair down around her shoulders, hoping it would help keep her cool, and then, when that did no good and she still felt like she might spontaneously combust, she walked into her kitchen and popped open her trusty freezer, then closed her eyes as the cool air hit her skin.

"Yes, baby, that's it. Right there."

An all-too-familiar chuckle hit her ears and she glanced over quickly before resuming her position in front of the freezer, frozen steaks be damned.

"You know, Bec, you could just run your A/C like a normal person." Nick closed her front door. "And lock your damn door. I could be a serial killer or something."

Becca peeked one eye open at him. "Are you?"

"Not usually, though after the day I've had, my brothers might make the list."

"I sense a story there."

She closed her eyes again and ordered her heart to ignore the man before her, to slow down. It was running away like a crazy thing in her chest, doing nothing more than elevating her temperature, and she was already hot enough.

"Isn't there always a story these days? But before we go there, what's up with the freezer treatment?"

"It was insane at the diner today, the kitchen running wild and burning me up. I tried to cool off on the ride home with the windows down and all, but it's still so dang hot outside, so all the windows let in was more hot air. Then I tried to take a cold shower, but you know I'm a chicken and couldn't manage it. So now I'm here."

Nick walked by her, his arm grazing her back in a quick hello, and Becca clenched her eyes shut as a tingly feeling worked through her from the spot he'd touched, out through the rest of her, until she was a buzzing, numb mess. Like always around him. By now she would have expected her body to become immune to Nick, but after more than twenty years, instead of her wanting him less, she wanted him more. It was pathetic and ridiculous, and did she mention pathetic? But there it was.

He opened the fridge side, pulled out a beer, and closed it, then sat down on one of the barstools. "You know you have A/C in your car, too, right?"

"Uses extra gas."

"So?"

"So, King Hamilton, I'm not in the habit of wasting money by using extra of anything."

At the insult, Nick's eyes dropped to his beer, and she felt like crap. "I'm sorry."

"You should be."

"Well, I'm hot."

A smile played at his lips as his eyes slowly slipped down her body and then back up, sending a fresh wave of sparks and silly hope working through her. "Yes. Yes, you are."

"Shut up."

"Yes, ma'am."

"What are you doing here anyway?"

At that, Nick took a long pull of his beer, and Becca's brow creased. "What happened? You said you were ready to kill your brothers."

"Nothing really. Same old stuff."

"I know that tone." She closed the freezer and then, missing its wonder, she fanned herself with her tank top. "It's time I reconsider a move up north, but then snow and driving in snow."

"Yeah, that'd be pretty dangerous with your track record."

She continued to fan herself. "What? It was one mailbox, not the whole street."

"Two mailboxes."

"All right, fine. Two. But I bought them replacements." She grabbed a flyer from her stack of mail, folded it in half, and used it as a makeshift fan. "Ahhh."

"What are you, menopausal or something?"

She pointed at him. "Watch your mouth, boy." He laughed, the sound so glorious she almost closed her eyes again so she could bask in it, but then that would be all sorts of awkward, and Becca tried to maintain her cool around her best friend. Even if right now she was anything but cool in every sense of the word.

"Now spill it."

Becca pulled out a bottle of water and leaned a hip against the counter.

"You could at least drink with me."

"It's five thirty. I like to keep my alcoholic tendencies for night-time hours."

"It's P.M. That stands for nighttime."

"Wow. Is that what that Ivy League education of yours taught you? 'Cause you might want to ask for a refund. At least a partial, right? Because night starts with an *N*, not a *P*, and time starts with a *T*, not an *M*. And, in fact, P.M. stands for post meridiem, so you can send me that money they give you for the refund."

"All right." Nick pulled out his wallet, counted out several bills, and tossed them onto the counter. "Now go turn on the damn A/C. It's hot in here."

With a loud, long, and drawn-out sigh, Becca pushed the money back toward him. "You know I'm not taking that."

"Well, I'm not taking it back, so take it or burn it." He shrugged. "It's nothing to me."

"See that right there? That's why you can't get a solid date. No girl wants a guy who burns money. I mean seriously. Not only is that six shades of insane, but hello, fire hazard, right?"

He cracked a smile and she grinned back, lost in those amazing blue eyes, crystal clear even through his glasses. Years and years around him and she still couldn't pinpoint the exact shade. They were sky blue with flecks of navy and turquoise. They were perfect . . . he was perfect.

And now she'd drifted into lala land again.

"Now that you're less jerk-ish, can you tell me what's going on?"

Nick fiddled with his beer bottle while she walked over to the wall unit, tapped the gauge from 78 to 75. That was the best she could do, and even that small drop made her cringe.

"Thank you, Madame Cheap."

"You're welcome, Sir Spend-a-Lot. Now can you tell me what happened?"

"An investor came by the office today."

"The Lexington office?"

"Yeah, surprise visit. Or at least a surprise for me."

"So they just showed up? Who do they think they are? And do they know who you are? I mean, you don't just show up to meet with Nick Hamilton. That requires special contacts and appointments months and months in advance. Even then he might be too busy to show."

He laughed now and joined her on her couch, loosening up into the Nick she adored so much. "Actually, it wasn't a total surprise visit. Trip and Alex set it up, driven by Trip no doubt. Alex would never ambush me like that. Plus, they weren't even there, just me looking like a dumbass."

"Damn."

"I know."

"Well, what did you say?"

Nick smiled as he took another sip of his beer. "To get the hell out."

"You didn't."

"Basically. And then I called Trip and told him he could screw himself. That I was the one who did everything for Dad, that it was my business, not theirs."

At that Becca cleared her throat and became very interested in the wrapping around her water bottle, which had a small tear in it just begging to be torn wider. These sorts of imperfections were Becca's undoing.

"Say it."

"What?" She continued to work the tear until it sliced across the wrapper, and then that looked positively silly so she had to pull the wrapper off completely. Now there was just that annoying glue line . . . and avoiding Nick's question.

"Whatever it is you're thinking. I can practically hear you already and you haven't said a word."

Becca turned to him and crossed her legs up under her like a five-year-old, the way she always sat. God, no wonder Nick couldn't see her as anything but a friend. She acted like a tiny child, not at all like a thirty-three-year-old should act.

"I'm listening."

"Well, it's just that it is their business, too. And I know you did everything for Carter, but he was their dad, too. I just think before you yell at them, you should hear them out."

Nick shook his head, fuming already. "You agree with them, don't you?"

"No. I don't think they should have scheduled a meeting with the investors without telling you. Especially without having the balls to show. That was wrong. Way wrong. But they love you. And you love them. This isn't something that should separate your family. I mean, I can't stand Reagan half the time, but she's my sister. Family matters, and you don't shut them out. You talk."

"There's nothing to say. They want to sell, I don't. We're at an impasse and they can't sell without my signature. There's no way in hell I'll give it. It's just . . ." He stared off into her small family room, and if she didn't know Nick so well, she might have been embarrassed.

It was cozy in an affordably chic kind of way. She'd had her uncle install hardwoods a few years ago, had painted just last year, and her curtains and wall hangings were cute. But still, his apartment in Lexington was so much nicer than her tiny ranch house, and forget his house over at the Hamilton farm. Two of her houses would fit inside his house. Her house might have been nice enough when it was built in 1987, but it hadn't aged especially well, and though she'd made updates after her grandmother died and left the house to her, it was still an old house.

"You know you don't have to decide today." She reached out and took his hand, and he immediately threaded his fingers through hers. They'd held hands like this plenty of times over the years, but after his father died, she'd found him holding on for longer, like he needed a bit of her strength.

"It's just . . . Trip said something that's stayed with me, and now I wonder if I'm really holding on for myself rather than the good of the company"

"What did he say?"

"He said the staff aren't as happy as they used to be. Like I'm some brooding boss, making everyone's life miserable. Am I a brooding boss?" His blond locks fell over his glasses, his mouth set in a half frown, and it took everything in her not to wrap her arms around him and hug him until that frown turned into a smile again.

"No. Well, maybe a little. But it's only natural. You lost your father."

"Five years ago."

Becca shrugged. "Still hurts. Years don't erase the pain."

He finished off his beer. "Yeah, but I should be dealing with it better. Over it by now."

"Says who? There's no expiration date on bereavement. Memories last a lifetime, and those memories can burn like a hot iron when you know there's no reliving them."

"I think that's the real reason I don't want to sell. If I sell, then it's like he's really gone."

"But, Nick . . . he *is* gone. Selling or not won't change that fact. It sucks and I wish with all my heart it weren't true, but it is, and you can't keep living your life by the code of WWCD."

"WWCD?'

"You know—What Would Carter Do?"

Nick rolled his eyes. "You are never going to let me live that down, are you? It was one summer, one WWJD bracelet. They were trendy."

"So were fanny packs, but you didn't see me wearing one."

He chuckled softly. "Touché, though I think you'd look hot as hell in a fanny pack."

"Yeah, not happening, but don't you think it's funny that 'hot as hell' is meant as a compliment when 'you look like hell' is an insult? I mean, what's that about? It's interesting, right?"

"No, not even a little bit."

Now it was Becca's turn to laugh. "Want to stay for dinner?"

"Nah, I want to go out."

Suddenly, Becca remembered what Alex and Kate had hinted at earlier, and she pulled her hand free from his, ignoring the confusion that crossed his face. "Right. Alex and Kate mentioned something about that."

"About what? Wait, when did you see Alex and Kate?"

"They were at the diner this morning."

"Ah."

"Yeah."

"So you don't want to go get something to eat? I'll buy. Just in case you forgot, I'm loaded." He flashed her that Crest commercial smile of his.

"Loaded with arrogance. But seriously, what about . . . ?" Becca trailed off, hoping Nick would fill in the gap, but all he did was cock his head.

Though, really, did it matter if he were seeing someone? They were friends. And friends had dinner together all the time. It was fine, natural, but then why didn't he tell her that he'd met someone, and why didn't he go to this new chick's house to talk out his issues instead of hers? And why hadn't he introduced her to this woman? Or maybe he was embarrassed to introduce Becca, the waitress, to what was sure to be a fancy, rich kind of lady.

"Bec?"

"What?"

"Dinner?"

"Right." Becca swallowed hard and tried to push aside the ache in her chest, the sadness working its way through her stomach. "Sure. Just let me change."

Nick thumbed the hem of her shorts. "Why? I like those. They're like bathing suit bottoms or something."

Becca swatted his hand. "Shorts, asshole. They're called shorts."

"Whatever you say."

"I'm changing for sure now."

Nick huffed loudly and made a show of getting up. "All right, all right. I'll help you get undressed. You don't have to yell at me about it."

Becca grinned and pushed him back down. "You are so stupid."

"You love me."

"I do," Becca said.

If only you knew how much.

* * *

Nick placed a hand on the small of Becca's back as he led her through Ray's Crab Shack, one of their favorites, and apparently the busiest place in town.

He'd seen Becca in plenty of dresses, but after watching her in front of that freezer door, wearing that tiny tank top and those barely there shorts, he was struggling to keep from touching her. Which was ridiculous, not to mention dangerous.

Becca was his best friend, he adored her, but he couldn't deny that Becca had turned into a beautiful woman, with curves in all the right places and the kind of rich, olive skin of Brazilian models. Couple that with her long, brown and caramel wavy hair and green eyes, and Nick had to force himself not to stare.

Plus, the looks she kept getting around the restaurant were enough to cause his alpha side to take over. She might not be his, but she wasn't theirs . . . at least not yet.

He ignored the pang in his chest at the thought of Becca with someone else, married off, no longer his whenever he needed her. He knew he was a selfish ass for wanting to monopolize her time, but he needed her friendship too much right now to lose it.

Thankfully, Becca had only had two real relationships, one of which had ended just a year ago, and even those were short. Nick didn't really know why she wasn't already married or why she refused to date a guy for long, but he wasn't complaining.

"Want to sit outside?"

Becca's gaze fell on the back deck. "You remember the freezer incident, right?"

"Come on. There's a nice breeze coming off the lake tonight. If you get hot, we'll move."

Her gaze switched to Nick, then the overly crowded restaurant, where Nick would have to pay attention to how he acted around Becca or else land her in the thick of Hamilton family gossip, and he didn't want to deal with that tonight. Right now, he wanted to lose himself in one of their crazy conversations, have a few beers, and forget the rest.

"Fine, but you're buying me one of those fruity drinks to make up for it."

He grinned. "Fruity drink coming up." Nick tapped the shoulder of the waitress walking in from outside. "We'll have a Miller Lite and a piña colada out here."

"All right, Nick," the waitress said with a smile. "Anything else you need?"

"No, that's fine. Thanks."

The door closed behind her, and Becca and Nick continued around to a table by the railing, overlooking the expansive lake that was as calm and clear as possible tonight. A pang of regret moved through him as he remembered all his fishing trips out there, the competitions he'd entered and won, how close he'd been to being so much more than the person he was today.

But then, was that really the life he'd want if he had a family? Traveling all the time, never a solid income beyond his inheritance and earnings from Hamilton Industries and Stables?

No.

Plus, he'd never feel right earning money from the Hamilton businesses just because his last name was Hamilton. He had to work for what he earned.

"What was that about?" Becca asked, pulling his attention back to the moment.

Nick glanced around. "What'd I miss?"

"That waitress. She was very nice." Becca's eyebrow was cocked, and she was staring at Nick like she was hoping he'd give her the missing piece to some complex puzzle.

"Um, I guess so. Look, what do you think of—"

"But you know her, right?"

"I've seen her before, sure. What's this about?"

At that, Becca stared out over the water. "Nothing. Just trying to figure something out." She bit her lip and Nick's attention switched to her mouth, curious what it would be like to kiss that mouth. Would she taste all sunflowers and summer air, the way she smelled, or would he find something totally different—totally new? He'd found his mind drifting there more times than he could count lately, which meant he needed to put an end to his self-imposed drought before his hormones made him do something crazy. Like hit on his best friend.

But truthfully, drought or not, it had always been hard to ignore his attraction to Becca. After all, she was a woman—a very, very attractive woman—and she was smart and funny and her smile could stop him in his tracks. She was—

He shook his head before his thoughts could travel anywhere else. *Pull yourself together, man.*

"She's a waitress, Bec."

Her gaze snapped back over to him. "So am I."

"I didn't mean it like that. I mean, she works here. I've seen her before here, but I don't know her. Do you? Is that why you're asking?"

"No. I just . . ."

"What?"

"Well, Alex and Kate mentioned something, and I'm just curious why you haven't told me yourself." She stared at Nick pointedly, almost like he was in trouble, but he couldn't for the life of him figure out what he might have done.

The waitress in question brought over their drinks and smiled wide as she asked for their order.

"We'll both have the crab cakes."

She eyed Becca like she wanted to make sure he wasn't ordering for her without her permission, but Becca and Nick had ordered the same thing everywhere they went for years. They'd learned a long time ago that if they didn't, they'd only want whatever the other one had and end up switching plates, so they'd made an agreement to get the same thing and save each other the whole spectacle.

"That's it." Becca's eyebrows went up again and the waitress's eyes fell on Nick, and Becca repeated, "I said that's it. We're done ordering."

Nick's gaze traveled back to his best friend in confusion. "What was that?"

"She was staring at you like you're a celebrity."

"Well, I am. Didn't you hear? I'm the reason they put in that traffic light on Green and Main. They should build a monument in my honor."

Becca laughed, the moment easier to sit in, but Nick had to wonder where this was coming from and why it sounded a hell of a lot like jealousy. But Becca had never once hinted at any interest in Nick. There was an unspoken agreement between them that they couldn't go there, and neither of them had—despite Nick's thoughts drifting there more often than they should.

"So, like I was saying, did you watch Crazy Cane's latest on chemtrails?"

Crazy Cane was an anonymous YouTuber who videoed all kinds of conspiracy theory things, then uploaded them to his channel of millions of subscribers like Nick and Becca, who both loved a good conspiracy theory.

"You're such a nerd."

"So are you and you know it. Now, did you watch it?"

She leaned in closer. "You know I did. The question is why would the government spray crap all around the sky for no good reason?"

Nick matched her lean. "It isn't for no good reason. It's to hide whatever would have been seen. They're keeping something from us."

"Did you hear what you just said?"

"I did. Look, I'm not in business mode right now. Give me a break."

"Well, can you at least try for English?"

Nick laughed as he rose up to take a drink from Becca's straw. Her gaze hit his, and he realized how close he was to her. If he moved a few inches, his lips wouldn't be on her straw—they'd be on her mouth.

Swallowing, because clearly his beer was hitting him too quickly, he cleared his throat and sat back down. "It's good."

"It is, but they put too much rum in it, or whatever they use to make it. I'm going to pass out and you'll have to carry me to your car."

Nick's eyes danced with mischievousness. "But then how could you be sure I wouldn't take advantage of you?"

"Because you're you," a deep voice said from behind them, and Nick turned to see Trip and Emery standing there. "Care if we join y'all?"

Nick's jaw tightened. "It's a two-person table."

"We need to talk about this."

"Not here."

"Hey, Nick." Emery leaned down to kiss his cheek.

"Hey, Em. Doing okay?"

She smiled. "I am." Then she walked over and kissed Becca's cheek, too. "Hey, Bec."

Becca hugged her, and they all sat in awkward silence for a moment, before Becca nodded to the table beside them. "You can pull up that table." Nick glared at her, but all she did was glare right back.

"I thought you said y'all worked this out," Emery said to her husband.

"We did," Trip said.

Nick laughed sarcastically. "Right. How'd you know I was here anyway?"

"Saw your car."

Nick eyed Becca. "We should have taken your car."

"Still would have known it was you. You two are attached at the hip lately. If Becca's not at the diner, you're usually with her."

The back deck had filled up now, the evening crowd out, and the last thing Nick wanted was for them to hash this out in the open like this, with half the town's ears pricked for some good gossip. The brothers had agreed to maintain the Hamilton family image after their father died, avoid gossip, and make sure the town trusted them to continue the legacy. The last thing the Hamilton name needed was for the town to see the brothers arguing.

"Sit already before they start talking."

Trip released a breath, and Nick realized for the first time that his brother was nervous. A part of him thought *good, he should be*, but the other part felt bad. This wasn't how things should be between them. Trip handled Stables and Nick handled Industries and that was just how things went. Nick would never dream of trying to sell Stables without consulting Trip, and regardless of what his brother said, he knew a part of him felt guilty for stepping on Nick's toes.

"Can I get y'all something?" The waitress came back over, her gaze hitting Nick again before going to Trip and Emery, and he thought Becca might fly out of her seat. The thought made him smile despite his brother's presence.

"Sweet tea for me," Emery said.

Trip motioned to Nick's glass. "I'll have what he's having."

The waitress smiled at Nick. "I'd like what he's having, too."

"What does that even mean?" Becca said, and Nick grinned over at her as the waitress scooted off.

"Calm down, bulldog."

"She's ridiculous. I mean, own it, girl. If you want to give him your number, do it. Don't dance around."

Emery tapped her fingers against the table, her eyes twinkling as she peered at Becca. "I think there's only one woman Nick's calling these days." Then there was a loud thump from under the table, followed by, "Ouch. I didn't say anything."

"You're saying plenty." Trip shook his head at his wife, like she'd revealed some scandalous secret. And then Becca took a long sip of her piña colada, refusing to meet Nick's eye.

What the hell was going on? So what if Nick hung out with Becca all the time? It wasn't like this was something new. He'd been hanging out with her since they were kids, and losing his dad had done nothing more than confirm to him that she was the only person beyond his brothers who meant anything to him. And maybe the only person in the world who truly understood him. He'd hang out with her as much as he liked, outside opinions be damned.

"Anyway, what were y'all talking about?" Emery asked, attempting to change the subject.

"Chemtrails."

"What trails?" Trip asked. "Wait, is this that conspiracy theory nonsense again?"

Case in point. Becca would never call it nonsense because she believed all the crazy as much as he did.

"It's not nonsense," Becca said. "This guy films it all. You can't argue with evidence."

Nick's eyes fell on his friend, and he thought the rest of them could all go to hell. This was his person, the one who got him, and he got her, and that kind of friendship didn't have to be explained.

"So what's happening at the stables?" Nick asked, sure that mention of the farm would get Trip going on a tangent, and it did.

He started in on a few new stallions Alex had bought, new owners he was working with, and before long they'd eaten their crab cakes, finished their third round of drinks, and Becca was yawning.

"We should probably head on. Becca has an early day tomorrow." Her eyebrows rose in question because she had the day off, but Nick had taken all the niceties he could handle. He wanted to relax, and he could no longer do that with Trip around.

"Right, early day."

"All right, see you two later." Emery rose up and hugged Becca, then Nick, and Trip offered his hand for Nick to shake. But Nick knew his brother, and he knew that shake would serve as an unspoken agreement that he was okay with selling, okay with what Trip had done. So instead of taking his hand, he patted him on the back.

"We'll talk Monday."

"Nick . . ."

"Monday. I've had enough for today."

Trip nodded slowly, they said their good-byes, and finally Nick was outside the restaurant, breathing in the chilled night air, his mind fuzzy from the effort to sit beside his brother without starting an argument. He and Becca climbed into his BMW and he set off down the road, the quiet giving way to thoughts he didn't want to have—questions he didn't want to answer. Because at the end of the day, maybe Trip was right. Maybe it was time to sell.

"You okay?" Becca asked once they pulled down her driveway and were parked outside her house.

"Yeah, just thinking." Nick rolled his head toward her, and Becca opened her mouth to ask him something, but Nick's brain couldn't handle any more questions, any more thoughts. "See you tomorrow?"

Her mouth snapped closed and she glanced out the windshield. "Right. See you tomorrow, Nick."

Chapter Four

Becca woke to the sound of someone or something banging around in her kitchen. Immediately, she grabbed the baseball bat she kept beside her bed and started out the door. Thank God she hadn't woken up thirty minutes before to exercise like she'd planned or she might have been killed by the intruder.

She edged down the still-dark hall because the sun wasn't fully awake either, and then jumped into the kitchen, only to scream and then listen as the person in her fridge screamed, and then the baby on said person's hip began to cry. Loudly.

"Reagan? What in the hell—?"

"Shhh!" her sister reprimanded, then pointed to the child sitting at Becca's kitchen table, her hands over her ears like earmuffs. Her light brown hair was parted down the middle and pulled up into two high pigtails that hung in curls, and she had the same olive complexion as most of the Starks.

"Oops, sorry, Anna banana." Becca dropped the bat on her couch and walked over to peck her niece's chipmunk cheek, then glared at her sister. "What are you doing here this early in the morning?"

"We're out of milk and Anna wanted cereal."

"Why are you out of milk?" Becca grabbed the gallon jug from her fridge, poured it over her niece's cereal, and then replaced it before turning on her sister, who was suddenly very interested in the kitchen sink. "Reagan?"

The sun's rays cast in through the window over the sink, highlighting shimmery tears, and Becca's heart sank. "What happened?"

"I can't talk about it here."

Becca motioned to the family room, which, with the open floor plan, wasn't much better, but it was a small house, what could she do? "Ty lost his job again, and my credit card was declined at the market yesterday. I don't know what we're going to do."

Reagan dried her tears with the back of her hand, then ran a hand over baby Cade's head, and the sucker in Becca sighed. "How much do you need?"

Reagan's face lit. "Seriously? You'll help us?"

As though Becca hadn't been the one to bail them out every single time Ty lost his job, which was pretty much every other week. Ty was the perfect example of why high school superstars don't matter. He was quarterback of Triple Run High, every girl in the school wanted him, and Reagan snagged him. But then, when Ty realized that his talents in a small town didn't translate to college and he was placed on special teams, then benched, he moved back home and drank his sorrows away.

What made it all worse was that Ty still thought of himself as a superstar and told stories of his best games to anyone who would listen. And Becca might feel bad for him, if it weren't that he treated her sister like it was all her fault and his children like they were nuisances.

Becca's mother had warned her against helping her sister, saying Ty put Reagan up to asking Becca and would take her for all she had if she wasn't careful, but Becca loved her niece and nephew. How could she let them suffer? It wasn't their fault they had crappy parents.

Though she only worked at the diner, Becca saved every dollar she made, so she had quite a savings by now. It all started with her obsession with Dave Ramsey years ago, and her determination to make the best of what she had. Then her grandmother died, and because Becca had been the one to care for her—and okay, the favorite—she left everything to Becca. Which wasn't much. But a house with no mortgage and twenty thousand dollars wasn't anything to sneeze at. So whenever Reagan came over, Becca always caved.

And her deep loathing for her brother-in-law grew still more.

"Reagan, maybe it's time you get a job and let Ty stay home with the kids." At her pointed stare, Becca sighed. "All right, so maybe not, but I bet Aunt Karen would agree to keep the kids while you work." Their aunt and uncle lived on the Stark property, too, which had been Becca's grandmother's. There were three homes there—one

Uncle Mark and Karen lived in, the other Reagan took over, and the last was Becca's house. The property was fifteen acres in total, and though that would normally feel like a fair amount of land, with the Starks Becca needed more like a hundred so she could breathe without her family always showing up.

Her parents had moved to Florida years ago, and though they visited from time to time, they were content in their bubble. Instead of coming back to Triple Run, which her mother had always hated, they insisted that Becca and Reagan visit them there. Which was the reason Becca had dropped out of college in the first place, to take over caring for her grandmother. No one else would step up to the plate, and Granny refused to move to Florida, so Becca had no choice.

Years later now, she still wondered for what might have been. What might have happened if she'd finished her degree, worked at a hospital or doctor's office, and maybe met and married a doctor husband of her own? But then her mind drifted to Nick, and she shook off the thought. Even if she'd finished her degree and training, her heart would always belong to Nick Hamilton.

After handing over sixty dollars and a check for five hundred more, Becca placed her hands on her hips in her best attempt at mimicking their mother. "This is for groceries. Understand? Don't you dare give a dollar of it to that POS husband of yours."

"Hey! He's not—" Becca cocked her head and her sister relented. "Fine, okay."

"What about clothes and stuff? Are they okay?"

Reagan eyed her kids affectionately. Though she had horrible taste in men, she loved her children. That much was clear. "I think they're okay. I was going to run to that consignment shop in Crestler's Key tomorrow and pick up a few things."

"I'll go."

"Are you sure?"

"Yeah, I'm off today."

They fell into an uncomfortable silence before, finally, Anna asked to go home and play with her cat. It was a stray kitten Becca had found wandering around behind the diner last week. At first, she'd brought it home, all gray and white and full of fear, telling it that she would give it a good home. And she'd planned to do just that. Until Anna walked into her house and squealed with excitement, and

Becca handed over the kitten and everything she'd bought it, her heart happy.

"Please, Mommy," Anna said again. "Mittens is probably crying for me."

"Mittens? I thought her name was Ramsey."

Reagan deadpanned, "Seriously? You named the cat after a financial guru?"

"Hey," Becca said with mock offense. "Dave is a genius."

"Mommy . . ."

Shaking her head at her sister, Reagan lifted Cade higher on her hip. "You are such a dork."

"Well, at least this dork can buy milk."

"Hey, that's not fair."

"I'm sorry," Becca said with a fake frown.

"No, you're not."

"Okay, I'm not. But it's because I think you deserve better."

Reagan released a long breath. "I know, I know. All right, little bits, let's go. I love you, big sister." She hugged Becca's neck, and Becca kissed Cade's head before walking over to hug her niece tight.

"You can spend the night with me next Saturday if you want. Movie and popcorn?"

The little girl bounced, her curly pigtails bouncing along with her. "Really?"

"It's a date." Becca kissed her cheek, then waved them all good-bye.

She had just started to close the door when a hand reached out to stop her. "Good God, what now?" Becca opened the door, only to startle back.

"Man, Bec, is that the greeting you give everyone at seven thirty in the morning or just me?" Nick flashed her that grin she loved, and a part of her wondered what it would be like to be able to lean in to kiss him. To feel his arms around her. To snuggle against his chest.

"Bec?"

She shook her head to clear it. She needed coffee, stat.

"What are you doing here?" she asked.

"I noticed your car looked dirty."

Becca stared at him. "And . . . that's new how?"

Nick ran a hand through his hair. "Fine, I wanted to get out of the house. Trip kept calling me to talk about the offer, and then Alex came over and I had enough. So I told them I had to get over here to help you with something."

"And that something is my dirty car?"

For the first time, Becca noticed the wash bucket and cleaning supplies in Nick's hands. "What did you bring over, everything you own?"

"No, of course not. I stopped at the Ace on the way over."

"That's like a hundred dollars' worth of stuff."

Nick shrugged and Becca glared at him.

"What? I'm trying to be nice here."

Becca opened her mouth to tell him that there were people out there, people a house away, who couldn't afford to buy groceries and he was throwing money away on her stupid car. But then she thought it wasn't fair to hold his wealth against him. He was a generous man, constantly donating to charities and events around Triple Run. He was rich, but he wasn't showy about it.

At least not usually. She eyed the impressive display of cleaning supplies. "So we're cleaning?"

Nick grinned. "Go get changed. I'll make you coffee."

Nick watched Becca sashay down the hall, his gaze traveling to the hem of her nightgown, barely covering her ass, and he had to clench his jaw to keep from following her to her room for a morning of something very different from washing a car. But then he thought about his brothers, and how Becca was the only person in the world he trusted anymore, the only one who truly understood him, and he forced himself to turn away instead, the screen door hitting loudly on his way out.

The sun wasn't fully out yet, like his half-dressed friend inside, and as he breathed in the crisp morning air, he took the opportunity to scan Becca's yard. Ancient Toyota Highlander parked in the carport, the azaleas perfectly trimmed by the house. Around back he would find the same porch swing and hand-painted pots overflowing with plants, the small vegetable garden, and then the rest was just grass. Grass that should have been cut a week ago and was likely driving Becca crazy. She liked to keep everything in perfect order, but time wasn't always on her side—or money.

Nick thought of the lawn service that handled all of the farm, including his house, and decided he would add one more stop to their rotation, Becca's stubbornness be damned. She could consider it payment for putting up with him all these years.

"Where are we doing this?" The screen door hit against its frame, and Nick turned, only to do a double take at what Becca was wearing. Or rather how little. His eyes swept quickly down her sports bra and barely there shorts, before snapping back up to her eyes. Thank God he had transition lenses on his glasses, or else she'd know exactly what he was thinking right now.

"What are you wearing?" he asked.

She eyed her outfit. "Did we have the conversation about me burning up yesterday or not? If we're washing my car, I'm going to make sure I'm comfortable. Besides, I might work out after." Nick cocked his head, and she threw up her hands. "Fine, I won't. But it was this or a bikini, and I figured I'd take it easy on you." She winked at him, and he had to order his throat to swallow because suddenly all he could think about was Becca and a bikini and how the hell he could convince her to go back inside and change into said bikini.

He was pathetic.

"Nick?"

"Hmmm? Oh, right. Have your keys?"

"They're in the ignition."

He grumbled as he headed toward the carport. "You don't lock your front door and you leave your keys in your ignition? What is wrong with you?"

A grin played on Becca's lips. "Plenty, but not nearly as much as is wrong with you, so zip it or I'll go back in and you can handle this car-washing business all by your lonesome."

The grumbling turned to laughing, and Nick thought how often that were the case around Becca. Within moments in her presence, he was smiling or laughing, relaxed. "Fine, consider me zipped."

"I'll get the truck, you go fill the bucket."

"All right, but I have to head to Crestler's Key today, so I don't have all day for this. None of your obsessive detailing. And no wax."

Nick stared at her. "There'll be wax."

"Nick, come on. You know I don't care."

"Just because you don't doesn't mean you shouldn't."

"What? Nobody on the planet could follow that line of thinking, especially not at seven thirty in the morning and only one cup of coffee in her."

Sure the conversation was going nowhere, Nick continued on toward the carport, calling over his shoulder, "And what are you doing in Crestler's Key?"

Becca waved to her car. "Get the car first and then I'll explain."

With reluctance, Nick opened the driver's side door and slid the seat back to accommodate his height, then shut the door, and Becca's scent washed over him, clouding his mind for a moment. Damn, when did he start noticing things like Becca's smell? Surely that wasn't normal?

Shaking himself from the trance, he backed the car out of the carport and then drove over to where Becca stood beside the large oak in her front yard. "The car is here, now explain the Crestler's Key business."

"Since when are you all Triple Run pride and nothing else? That feud between Crestler's Key and Triple Run was ages ago. Who cares about it now?"

"Everyone cares."

"Not me."

Nick turned on the water, filled the bucket with more soap and water, earning an annoyed look from Becca, and tossed her a wash glove. "Don't let them hear you say that in town or you'll get exiled."

"If only."

Nick's hand froze on the hood of the car, and he peered over at her. "You want to leave?"

"I don't know. Maybe someday. Sometimes I feel like I've done everything here and I need to leave so I can do something new. Live a little."

"What about finishing nursing school?"

He couldn't see her expression from where she worked on the opposite side of the car, but by her silence he guessed that wasn't in the cards.

"Maybe someday," she said finally. "For now, I just want to do something. That's actually why I'm going to Crestler's Key. Well, to pick up some things for the kids, but also . . ." She trailed off and Nick stood up and walked around to her.

"Also what?"

"Since when are you so demanding?"

"Since birth. Since when are you so shady?"

Becca turned away from him, and he got the feeling he was missing something important, but he couldn't figure out what. "I don't know. I just . . ."

"Bec, tell me."

"Ugh, fine. I signed up for scuba diving lessons. To get certified."

Immediately, Nick burst into laughter. "Scuba diving? You?"

"Hey, I could do it."

"Do you remember that time we were at the park and you tried to shoot a basketball into the hoop and hit Mayor Phillips in the face instead?"

Becca scowled. "He was sitting right under it!"

"He was sitting in a bench halfway across the park."

"Well, that doesn't mean a thing."

Nick went back to soaping the car, a smile still on his face. He was methodical about it—too methodical, Becca would say—but he liked monotonous activities like this, activities where he didn't need to think. Or see his brothers. "It means you're the least athletic person on the planet, and if you go scuba diving, you'll likely drown. I can't allow that, now can I? Who would listen to me bitch about everything all the time?"

"Then you could just hire a shrink and sit on one of those fancy couches."

"And explain how my corrupted childhood has turned me into an asshole?"

"And analyze why your favorite color is black."

Nick straightened. "What's wrong with black? It's sophisticated."

"It's morbid. People choose *colors* for favorite colors."

"Black is a color; ask Crayola."

At that, Becca rolled her eyes and placed her hands on her hips in that sassy way she did when she was about to lecture him. He loved it and couldn't help but grin. "Black is the opposite of color. It's depressing, and besides, you look terrible in black."

"Listen, woman, no need for insults." Nick turned the hose on Becca, spraying her once, before holding the sprayer up like a gun. "Say you're sorry."

She glared at him with the intensity of a raging fire. "Hit me with that again and you're dead, Hamilton. Dead."

"You and what army? I've got a foot on you, plus all these muscles." He tugged off his shirt and flexed dramatically, laughing, until he caught Becca's expression as she took him in. Her eyes widened a touch and she swallowed, her clenched fists relaxing as a brief flicker of something that looked a lot like attraction crossed her face.

But then she cleared her throat and looked away, and before Nick could process what had just happened, she dashed for the soap bucket. "You spray me and I dump this on you."

He grinned. "Then it's a good thing I took off my shirt. I don't have a change of clothes, so unless you want to see the full frontal, I suggest you not." He knew she would redden at his words, but he didn't expect her gaze to flicker down and then back up to his face, her eyes darkening. God, was it possible she'd had the same thoughts he'd had about them? Surely not. He flirted with her all the time, but she never hinted at anything more, never said anything to suggest she'd thought about him as more than her best friend. So what was with all these looks?

Sure he needed to do something or else they might not survive the tension building between them, he flashed her one more grin and said, "You can just call this lesson one of scuba diving: remember to breathe."

"What the—?"

But before she could finish, he turned the sprayer on her, drenching her from head to toes and, good as her word, she tossed the bucket of soapy water at him, the suds hitting him square in the face and then sopping down his chest and shorts.

"I didn't think you would do it!" Nick removed his glasses and shook out his hair.

"I told you I would. Dammit, I'm drenched." She stomped her foot, but all she managed to do was splash herself from the puddle that had collected at her feet.

Nick cracked a smile and she pointed at him. "Don't you dare." Surrendering, he held up his hands, his eyes on her, covered in water, her hair hanging in drenched waves around her shoulders, and her hands on her hips in aggravation, and he thought she might just be the most beautiful thing he'd ever seen.

"Hot shower?" he asked.

"With you? No, thanks; you'd probably turn the water to cold on me."

"I didn't say with me, but hey, if you're offering, I'm not denying."

Becca shook her head, but she was smiling at him now. "Let's finish this. I have to leave in an hour."

"For the scuba diving lesson?"

"Yes, Mr. Sarcastic. I can do this."

Nick bit his lip and went to work on the side of her car, then resigned that he really couldn't let her go into a giant ocean with some half-assed instructor who knew shit about diving, he said, "I'll take the lessons with you. Are they on Saturdays, then? Six weeks or something?"

"Yes, but no, you're not. You're already certified."

He shrugged. He and his brothers were all certified when they were teens, back when their father used to take them on dive trips and they used to act like a real family, instead of whatever disjointed bunch they were now. "So? They don't have to know that."

"You'll start interjecting Nickisms."

"What the hell is a Nickism?"

Walking around to the other side of the car, Becca bent down to scrub the tires with the same wash glove she'd used on the car. Nick cringed, but he knew better than to correct her, especially when he had new territory to cover and the last thing he wanted to do was piss her off to the point that she really wouldn't let him join in the lessons.

"I'm waiting here."

The sun had turned hot overhead, September proving every bit as hot as August, and Nick wondered if they were in for another overly warm fall. That would change things a bit for the fall festival, and he made a mental note to talk to Trip about it because he was on the board of trustees for Triple Run.

If he started talking to his brother again.

Becca stopped in front of him. "You know, that know-it-all thing you do. Whatever it is, you know something about it. There's no way you can sit in a class, listen to some 'half ass' teach without you interjecting."

Crossing his arms, Nick plucked the wash glove from her hands just as she started to press it back to the car. "You just washed the tires with that thing. You can't touch the paint with it now."

"Why?"

"It'll scratch it."

Becca pointed at him. "See? That right there. A Nickism in the wild, ladies and gentlemen." She turned, her arms out, and then directed at him like he was part of a circus act. "You can't do anything without spewing Nickisms all over it."

"You know, that sounds a little dirty. What kind of Nickisms are we talking about here?"

She rolled her eyes and he tried to feign seriousness. "I take offense. I can sit in a class and keep my mouth shut."

"Fine; prove it. You can go to the class today, but if you issue even one Nickism, you're out of there."

Nick held out his hand and Becca glanced down before pressing her small hand into his large one. Immediately, warmth spread from the point of contact, up his arm, settling in his core, and it took every bit of his willpower not to tug her toward him, drenched and all, his lips crashing against hers, that sunflower and sunshine smell of hers washing over him.

God, he was in trouble.

"Deal."

Nick grinned. "Now about that hot shower . . ."

Chapter Five

"Stop it." Becca pushed her friend's shoulder and Nick scoffed. "I didn't say anything."

"You were thinking it."

Nick spun around, his arms out. "Do you see where we are? It's an elementary school. I'm supposed to master scuba diving surrounded by Elmo and Dora?"

"So what? I bet Elmo and Dora could teach you a thing or two. And besides, it's just the classroom portion. We'll move to the water in a few weeks."

Nick stopped walking beside a statue of a Native American chief with a cheesy smile on his face. "Mr. Chief here wants to know how we're supposed to learn to dive in a classroom."

"How did you learn?"

"My dad threw me into our pool with a mask and snorkel on, threw a pair of fins at me, and ordered me to go underwater or drown."

"Be serious."

Nick laughed. "Fine. We had a private instructor."

"Of course you did," Becca grumbled. Then she found the right classroom and opened the door, only to close it again and point to her friend. "Remember your promise."

Nick pretended to lock his lips and then passed the pretend key to Becca.

"And no mocking facial expressions."

"Hey, now, we said nothing about mockery. The instructor could be an eighty-year-old man carrying around an oxygen tank. How am I supposed to keep from smiling at that?"

Unable to keep from smiling herself, Becca pushed into the room, only to stop short, causing Nick to run into her. "Holy hot." Her gaze landed on the man at the front of the classroom, dressed in a fitted black T-shirt that showed every one of his perfectly cut arm and chest muscles. Dark brown hair shot off his head in spikes, and black ink climbed down from his biceps to his forearms.

"Hey there," Mr. Unbelievably Hot said, but Becca could only manage to sigh in reply.

"Jesus. I didn't know you were capable of drooling so much," Nick said, walking around her and starting for the back.

"Let's sit up front." Becca motioned to the front row, and Nick glanced at the instructor.

"Seriously? That's your thing?"

Becca took the middle seat and patted the desk beside her. "Honey, *that* is every woman on the planet's thing."

"I didn't think you were so typical."

"I'm typical when it comes to tattoos."

She grinned at the instructor and he grinned back, and Becca thought scuba diving lessons might have been the best idea she'd ever had.

Once the instructor looked away, Becca glanced around the classroom. Immediately, her thoughts drifted back to her and Nick's days in elementary school. They'd renovated over the years, but the feel of learning still hung in the air, ghosts of laughter from children running in the halls.

A memory popped up of Nick sitting in front of her and smiling wide as he attempted to pass her a stack of papers the teacher had handed to him as the row leader. Only the stack never made it into her hands. Their fingers hit as she reached for the stack and he tried to hand it off, and then they fell to the floor, white sheets scattering everywhere. It was that moment, him red and her laughing, that she knew they would be great friends.

"All right," the instructor said, bringing her back to the present. "It's three fifteen, so I think it's safe to say this is our class. I'm Zac Littleton and I'll be your instructor for the next six weeks."

"Littleton?" Becca asked. "Are you related to Kate?"

At that Nick finally looked up and at the instructor, and Becca caught the recognition cross his face. "You're one of Kate's brothers, right? I'm Nick Hamilton, Alex's brother."

"Right, I recognize you from the wedding." Zac walked over and shook Nick's hand, but whereas most men stiffened or appeared in awe when meeting one of the insanely wealthy Hamiltons, Zac seemed undeterred. There was something more to the way they stared at each other, a story Becca couldn't quite put together, and then she remembered the Hamiltons talking about another set of brothers in high school. Brothers from Crestler's Key who played baseball, competitors of theirs. Becca wondered if those brothers were the Littletons, but before she could dwell on it, Zac bit his lip and turned to her, and she had to fight to keep from giggling like a little girl.

Clearly, it had been a long, long time.

"And you are?"

"Becca Stark. I'm a family friend."

"Hmmm, too bad Kate hasn't introduced us yet. I'm sure I would have remembered you."

Becca grinned, and Nick cleared his throat loudly. "So, the class?"

"Right. Better get back to work." Zac winked at Becca, and she grinned back, embarrassed but unable to rein in her response to him. It had been a long time since she was this attracted to someone.

Well, someone other than unattainable Nick.

There were no more than twelve to fifteen students in total in the class, and Becca surmised that meant she would get plenty of time with hottie Zac, and maybe she could test the whole flirting and dating thing again in an effort to forget the guy beside her, who by all accounts saw her as nothing more than the tomboy next door.

"All right, first let's go over the basics. Scuba is actually an acronym for Self-Contained Underwater Breathing Apparatus, though people use it so frequently these days that *scuba* describes the sport without having to detail its meaning. And though you might worry about your athleticism, scuba diving is one of the easiest activities out there. Children as young as eight can be certified."

"Ha, see that. I'm good to go," Becca whispered, and Nick rolled his eyes.

"We'll see."

"What was that?" Zac's gaze fell on Nick, and Becca grinned wide as Nick's jaw ticked. It was so rare for Nick to openly dislike someone that she found it amusing. She'd like to test just how far that dislike could go, but she feared what Nick might say, and it was only the first day of class. Surely she could get in a few lessons before Nick got them kicked out.

"Did you have a question, Nick?"

"No, no question."

"Excellent, then do you think you could join me up here?"

Becca was on the verge of hysterics now as Nick glanced at her with wide eyes and a frown on his face. He wanted to make fun of the class, dis Zac as a "half ass," but it was all blowing up in his face.

"Go ahead, Nick," she urged.

With a quick glare at her, Nick slid out of his desk and stepped up to the front of the class. Instantly, Becca caught sight of someone behind her leaning forward for a better view, and she turned to see a pretty blonde, eyes locked on Nick, and Becca thought her interest was less in the lesson and more in the only eligible Hamilton left.

Zac motioned to the table behind him and the scuba diving equipment. "I'll go through each piece of equipment and the correct way to put it on using Nick as a dummy."

"Nick as a dummy," Becca mouthed and Nick's grimace deepened, only causing her to laugh harder.

"The most important pieces of equipment to consider first are your mask, fins, and exposure protection. Now we won't make Nick here change into a wet suit."

"You can," the blonde said. "We won't mind." She smiled and Nick grinned back, and suddenly Becca was the one frowning. What was she thinking, bringing Nick here where eventually they would all be in swimsuits? Was she trying to introduce him to his next date? Or maybe whoever his brothers had been hinting about had his attention fully occupied.

A sinking feeling worked through her.

"The most important thing about the mask is that it fits snuggly." He handed over a bright pink mask to Nick, who was very likely to kill Becca after this. "Go ahead. Try it on."

Nick held up the mask. "You're joking, right? This is way too small. And pink."

A smile played at Zac's lips, and Becca propped her chin up on her hand, enjoying the view of the two handsome men before her, each attempting to show their manliness. "It's an exercise, go with it," Zac said. "Unless you're not manly enough to wear pink."

"I'm manly enough. I'll own this pink." He attempted to slide the mask over his head and into place, fighting and struggling and grunting, but all he managed to do was get the mask onto his forehead, resulting in laughter from the class.

Zac chuckled beside him, and Becca thought Nick might shove

the mask at him. "Sorry, man, don't be mad. That was to illustrate a poorly fitting mask. Now try this one." Zac passed Nick a new mask and he easily slid it on, and hell if he didn't look all the more adorable as he grinned over at Becca. "Now the fins." Nick slipped on a pair, and then before long Zac had him completely dressed in scuba gear.

"Think this is funny, do you?" Nick asked around his snorkel mouthpiece, sending Becca into hysterics.

"Yes. Very. In fact . . ." She reached frantically for her bag and pulled out her phone. "Say cheese."

"Don't you—"

"Too late." She snapped picture after picture, before he finally waddled over to her and snatched the phone.

"All right, you can take it all off," Zac said.

"I can help him," the blonde called, and Becca ground her teeth together. She turned to tell her that he had help, but the woman was already by Nick, helping him remove each piece of equipment like she was slowly undressing him for things completely inappropriate in an elementary school classroom.

"Let's take a little break and then we'll go through the beginning steps."

Becca peered around to get a better look at the other people taking the class. It was half men and half women, all ages, and, like her, the women were all ogling their instructor and his assistant, Nick. She could only imagine how crazy they would go once they saw him in swim trunks or a wet suit.

Then her gaze turned to Zac, and she realized she'd get to see him in swim trunks or a wet suit, too. Maybe she could survive this after all.

Zac clapped at the front of the class, and everyone returned to their seats as he passed out various sheets of information on anything and everything related to diving. Finally, after half an hour of this and Becca's mind fuzzy from a thousand details she felt sure she'd never remember, he said, "I think that'll do it for today. Same time next week? We'll let you all dress up like Nick here." He patted Nick's back and Nick stiffened.

"Stop it," Becca mouthed, and he shook his head a little.

"The class after next, we'll take to the pool. Remember, you have to complete the online training before that class or you can't get in the water."

Everyone thanked him, and Nick stopped in front of Becca's desk, his mouth open to say something just as Zac stepped in front of them. "Sorry about that, man. Hope I wasn't too rough on you." He laughed, and Nick fake laughed back. Ah, the male ego at its finest.

"Nah, this isn't my first rodeo."

Zac's eyebrows lifted. "You're certified?"

Nick stood taller. "Certified at twelve. Been diving ever since, though it's been a few years since my last dive."

"So why are you taking the class?" Zac's eyes drifted to Becca and back to Nick. "Oh. I didn't realize you two were—"

"We're not." Becca stood quickly, narrowly bumping into Nick, which resulted in an annoyed head shake, but hey, she couldn't have the only prospect she'd had in months thinking she was already taken.

But then Nick threw an arm around Becca territorially, and she thought she might kill him, friendship be damned. A woman had needs, and a man like Zac could absolutely meet those needs. "Nah, Bec's my bestie, and I didn't want her diving with an amateur."

"She wouldn't be with an amateur."

Nick sized Zac up and down. "No offense, man; I'm sure you're skilled. But I think I'll go through the training with her all the same."

"Even though you're certified?"

"Even though I'm certified." Nick's gaze leveled on Zac. "Is that a problem?"

Zac's eyes found Becca's then, and she felt sure her face was a thousand and one shades of red. Two thousand and one. She. Was. Going. To. Kill. Nick! What the hell was he doing? "Money is money, right? You want to pay for it, I'm not complaining."

"That's what I thought."

"All right, then. See you next week, Becca. Nick." He nodded to the overly domineering, half-crazy man beside Becca and then left the classroom. As soon as he was out of earshot, Becca turned on Nick.

"What the hell was that?"

"He was making a move on you. The instructor. On a student. I couldn't allow such morally depraved behavior."

Becca's head twitched. "Yet you let that blond chick flaunt her goods all over you."

Nick tossed up a hand. "Hey, I'm not the instructor and she's not my student. And besides, she just offered to help. I didn't ask her to.

Why didn't you help? Oh, that's right, you were too busy drooling over Instructor Z."

"He's Kate's brother. Shouldn't you be nicer?"

Nick considered it for a second, then shook his head. "Nah. Alex would've supported me on this."

"Alex? Your brother Alex? Mr. All Over Anything That Walked before meeting Kate? Yeah, I don't think so. Zac is his brother-in-law. I think he'd tell you that you were being an ass."

They were outside now, rain pouring down in sheets, soaking everything and further clouding Becca's thoughts and mood. "You can't just bully every guy interested in me. And I don't even think he was. He was just being nice."

"First, I don't bully *every* guy. And second, he wasn't being nice. Guys aren't nice. They only want one thing. Zac only wants one thing."

"That's ridiculous!"

"It's not. Every guy you've ever met wanted to get in your pants."

Becca was fuming now, her hands in fists at her sides so she wouldn't be tempted to deck him. How dare he? How dare he! "Really? Every guy? You're a guy. You want to get in my pants?"

"Hell yes! Every single time I see you!"

Nick jerked back. What had he just done?

"Um, what I meant to say was—I was just proving the point that—I didn't mean me, as in literally me."

"Right. Of course you didn't." Becca's eyes dropped to the floor, then to the rain. "Look, I've got to hit that consignment shop for Reagan."

"Bec . . ."

"It's fine. I get it."

"I didn't mean to . . ." Nick ran a hand through his hair, then over his face. "I don't know why I said that."

She stared at him as though she wanted to ask him a question, a question he didn't want to answer. Not today, not ever. But then she released a breath and tightened her hold on her bag. "I'll see you later, Nick."

And then, before he could say or do anything else to royally screw up this day, she darted into the rain, disappearing around the edge of the school and out of sight. He waited until her Highlander pulled out of the school parking lot before slowly walking to his car, careless of the rain. Or the water he'd trek into his car. Or anything other than the fact that he'd spent all his adulthood hiding his true desires for his best friend only to blurt them out in a fit of jealousy.

He was such an idiot.

Sure he needed a distraction, he did the only thing he could do when he felt as lost as he felt right that second—he headed to the office, where the silence and comfort of work could help him think.

It took less time than it should to get there, but as he pulled into the parking lot, his blood turned to ice. Because parked in his normal spot was Trip's truck and beside it was Alex's old Corvette, then to the left of that a black Mercedes with an out-of-state tag.

All the heat in his body dripped from his head down to his toes as he parked a few spaces away from the threesome, hoping he was wrong and that this wasn't a meeting at his office without him.

He unlocked the main door and hit the number three once in the elevator. Each second felt more painful than the last as the ice running through his veins thickened, making it harder and harder for him to move, to breathe.

Finally, the elevator doors opened and Nick exited to a dark floor. Dark except for a small light shining out from the farthest corner from the elevator. He started toward the conference room, only to stop as Trip's voice hit his ears, and then suddenly the cold in him turned to scalding rage.

Nick stepped into the doorway, not bothering to knock; after all, this was his office, his conference room. Sure enough, Trip and Alex were seated at the conference room table across from William Compton, who'd shown up in this very same room the day before. Hadn't Nick sent him away? Hadn't he told Trip that he wasn't interested? Hadn't he been clear?

"What's this?" Nick asked from the doorway, unwilling to enter the room, to enter whatever traitorous shit was going on there.

"Nick . . ."

"What the hell is this?"

"Let's discuss this outside," Alex said, standing.

"Let's discuss it right here. Right now. What the hell is this?"

Trip lifted his head. "You weren't willing to hear William out, and we felt there was more to be discussed before he left town. So here we are."

"Meeting behind my back."

"We're just discussing the offer."

Nick shook his head. "This isn't your decision."

At that, Alex walked over. "It isn't only yours either. We need to talk about this with open ears and truly consider the best course of action for the company and our employees. I don't think you're doing that right now, and if you stop to think about it, you'll see I'm right."

"No, there's nothing right about what you're doing here. Nothing right at all." Nick turned on his heels and stormed out, grateful that his brothers let him leave without a fight. Because right now he was too angry to have this conversation, too hurt, and he didn't like the direction his thoughts were headed. He had no idea what he might say, and though his brothers deserved to hear his rage, he didn't want to say something he couldn't take back.

Some words couldn't be unsaid, but in that moment he was praying that some could.

He needed Becca, and the last thing he wanted was to have started something with her that he couldn't and wouldn't finish. Besides, she wanted nothing more than friendship with him, so even if he'd said everything he was thinking, so what? It would mean nothing and do nothing other than destroy their friendship.

Still, the expression on her face before she left flashed in his head, confusing him. It was like she was disappointed, like she had hoped he wanted her the way Zac and every other man on the planet wanted her.

But what sense did that make? None; none at all.

Jumping back in his car and slamming the door harder than he should, he took off, eager to get some distance away from his brothers so he could think. He told himself he was going to drive around for a while, clear his head, but he tended to head one place when he felt this lost, and before he'd even realized what he was doing, he found himself pulling down Becca's road.

The rain had let up to reveal clearer skies, and as he parked, he contemplated leaving without getting out of the car. She was clearly upset with him, and he wasn't in a position to make anybody feel better about anything. So why was he there? Because he was a selfish asshole who needed her, and despite whether or not she wanted to see him, he'd come. Unannounced.

He should leave, and he was tempted to, until he saw Becca's form appear behind her screen door.

Resolved that he couldn't leave without saying something, he pushed out of his car and kept his head down as he started toward her. He couldn't look up and see the hurt on her face, not yet, not when he was so close to hightailing it out of there, and she deserved for him to be better than that. She deserved the best version of him.

Finally, he took the two steps up to her door and lifted his gaze at the same time she stepped outside. His eyes locked on hers, on the hurt there.

"I thought you were supposed to go shopping?"

"I no longer felt like it."

"Bec, I . . . I don't know what to say."

She crossed her arms. "You said a lot already."

"I'm sorry about Zac."

The hurtful expression deepened. "That's not what I want you to be sorry for."

Nick studied her, at the slight redness in her eyes. "Have you been crying?"

"No." She swiped under her eyes and then fidgeted with her T-shirt. "I just woke up."

"Just woke up?" He took a step closer. "You're lying. You've been crying. But why?"

She shook her head, her bottom lip trembling, and Nick wanted to cut out his own heart for causing her this pain.

"I didn't mean to do this. To upset you. I don't even know what I said. I mean the in-your-pants thing. I know that was crude and I shouldn't have said that. And of course you're more to me than that. You're my best friend. I would never . . ." He stopped as tears filled her eyes again. "Bec?"

"Can you just leave?"

He stared at her.

"Please. I'm not feeling well and I'm tired. I just want to curl up in bed and rest. I have to be at work early in the morning."

"I could stay, make you something?"

"No." Then she did the one thing he hated most. She put on a fake smile and tried to laugh, but no laugh had ever sounded less like

Becca's laugh. "You know you can't cook. Besides, I'm fine. Really. I just want to rest."

"So we're fine?" But even as the words left him, he knew the answer. They were anything but fine.

She swallowed hard and Nick wanted to pull her into his arms, stroke her hair, make her feel better in any way he could, do whatever she needed. "We're fine."

Right.

So why did Nick feel so much worse?

Chapter Six

Becca threw her hair into a high ponytail; then, frustrated with the way the elastic tugged at her hair, she pulled it down and instead piled her locks onto her head in a messy bun and wrapped the elastic around it before dropping her arms to her side.

It had been nearly twenty-four hours since Nick all but told her that he would never go there with her, never want more, and still, her heart ached as though he'd just said it. The confirmation that her feelings would never be returned made her want to call him and say she was done, throw in the towel, their friendship was too much for her.

But she cared about their friendship more than she cared about her heart, so she would lick her wounds, lock away her feelings, and move on. What else could she do?

"Bad mood?" Sage asked from the kitchen.

"Always," Becca joked, then grabbed the plates he'd set out and started for the table that had ordered the food. Thankfully, there were no Hamiltons in the diner that Sunday morning, or else she feared she might lose it.

So Nick didn't want in her pants. Wasn't that what she expected? Hadn't she known that all along? So why did it hurt so badly for her to hear it?

She could almost hear her heartbeat pick up speed when he said he wanted her every time he saw her, and a little part of her had pictured him sighing and pulling her into his arms, where he would kiss her with all the pent-up passion of a man who'd wanted her since the first moment he saw her.

They'd kiss and then kiss more, and then tell stories about how hard it'd been not to confess their undying love for the other and laugh about how long it'd taken them to get together. All would be well and fine and wonderful. Close book, happily ever after complete.

Instead, he took it all back, said he hadn't meant a word of it, then came by her house to reiterate just how much he didn't want her.

She still couldn't believe she'd let him see her crying, but she couldn't help it. It was either let him in or ignore him, which would only confirm that something was wrong. And while it hurt her tremendously to let it go, she had to. Nick was her best friend, and though her heart would forever be his in a different way, she didn't want to lose their friendship. It meant the world to her.

"Becca, new table." Willow motioned to the first table and she did a double take. Crap. Crap, crap, crap.

"Do you know them? You look pale."

"No, well, yes, a little. But I'm fine. Totally fine."

Only she was anything but fine.

Because seated at table one was none other than Instructor Zac and two other men who looked remarkably similar to him, which meant they must be his brothers. She thought she remembered meeting a slew of Littletons at Alex's wedding, but she'd forgotten that there were three brothers—and that they were quite this attractive.

"I can get it if you're busy," Willow said. "That's a full house of delicious over there."

Becca shook herself from her trance and waved off the waitress. "No, I'm good." Though Becca wished she could ignore them without being rude. The truth was that she didn't want Zac seeing her here, at work, where she was the bland waitress who would never amount to more.

A vision of the Becca she might have been flashed through her mind. Her as an ER nurse, and Zac coming in after some scuba diving accident, and her being the nurse to stitch him up. They would stare at each other while she worked, tension building. Instead, she was about to serve him coffee and pancakes.

Would you like extra syrup with that? No, me neither—but I'll give you my number if you ask.

God, she was pathetic. And all in an effort to put Nick out of her mind, which let's face it, was next to impossible.

"Hey there," she said as she neared. "I didn't realize teachers actually ate."

What the heck was that? Good God, it was no wonder she was single.

Zac turned and immediately a beautiful smile broke across his face. He was dressed in a long-sleeve Guy Harvey shirt, his hair spiking out as it had been the day before, and Becca wondered if he ever dressed nice, or if he, like her, preferred the ease of comfort clothes. "Becca, right?"

"Yeah. From scuba diving class."

He nodded, and the guy across from him piped up, "Damn, brother, I would have joined you for that training if I'd known this was what your students looked like."

Zac groaned. "Becca, this is my brother Charlie," he said, motioning to one of the other men with him. "And this dipshit is Brady. Feel free to file a harassment suit against him now. Trust me, he'll deserve it."

Brady grinned with pride. "Don't worry, I'll be a good boy if you want me to be. If not . . ."

He winked, and Zac tossed a sugar packet at him. "Leave her alone. Besides, she's taken."

"Is she now?" Brady studied her. "I wouldn't be surprised to hear it."

"Yeah, Alex's brother. Nick."

Becca waved her hands frantically. "Oh, no. No, she's not. And definitely not with Nick. He's a friend."

This seemed to please Zac and he turned to face her in the booth, suddenly very relaxed. "Now that's the most interesting thing I've heard all day."

She grinned back at him and set down their menus. "I'd love to stay and chat, but we're a little slammed."

"So you're taking dive lessons?" Brady asked, ignoring her attempt to leave.

"Yeah, on Saturdays. Do you all three teach or just Zac?"

"We own Southern Dive in Crestler's Key, so we teach throughout the year, whenever we're not on the farm."

Becca nodded. "I remember Kate saying she grew up on a farm. I didn't know y'all worked it, though."

"Yeah," Zac said. "We took over when our dad became too old to manage it."

"That's great that you can continue the family business."

"It can be." They stared at one another, and Becca bit her lip in an effort not to grin. She could get used to this kind of attention, even if a part of her felt sad that it was coming from someone other than Nick. Still, she needed to get used to the idea of someone else. Nick would never be a reality for her.

"Becca, order up," Sage called from the kitchen, and Becca turned back, waved that she was coming, then focused back on the Littleton brothers.

"Sorry. I've got to get to work."

"But you'll be back?" Zac asked, his voice tinged with a hope that sounded amazing after her encounter with Nick. See, some guys *did* want her. She was likable, maybe even lovable.

She grinned. "I'll definitely be back."

Becca walked around the rest of her tables to double-check drinks and ask if anyone needed anything, then grabbed the plates from Sage and went to deliver them to the giant table in the center of the diner, each chair full of trustee members.

"Here you go." Becca started handing out plates, then went to grab more, when she caught the conversation they were having.

"The fall festival is just three weeks away and we need confirmation of what the Hamiltons are doing. Where is Nick anyway? I thought he was going to meet us here?"

"I bet he's tied up with that new girl I overheard he was crushing on," one of them said.

"Oh, really? Who is that?" Charlotte asked yet another trustee who lived for gossip about the Hamiltons. She was every bit of sixty, married with her own lot of kids, but she had always hoped one of her daughters would marry a Hamilton.

"No idea. I didn't catch the end of the conversation. But I bet she's a lawyer or doctor or something fancy like him. Nick was always the smartest of the three. I bet that's where he is—with that lawyer or doctor."

"Actually, Nick's right here."

Becca glanced up to find Nick standing a few feet away from her, dressed in loose jeans and a light blue golf shirt, the look so perfectly Nicklike it made her heart clench tight. But the mayor and Charlotte were probably right. He was probably with whoever the new girl was, and because both Trip and Alex had mentioned something and now the trustees, clearly there was a girl. But then, why hadn't Nick mentioned the girl to her? Wasn't she his best friend?

"Hey," he said.

"Hey."

"Am I getting that plate in your hand, Becca, or are you going to keep holding it?" Mayor Philips laughed as he reached up, plucked a slice of bacon from the plate, and took a bite.

"Sorry, here you go, Mayor." Becca placed the plate in front of him, ignoring Nick because her mind really couldn't handle the man she wanted to want and the man she actually wanted being in the same space. Especially when one made it clear he wanted her back and the other made it abundantly clear he did not.

"Sit down, Nick," the mayor said. "We were just diving into the final details. Is Trip coming, too?"

"I think so." Nick stared after Becca, and she wanted to tell him to stop, to just sit down and they could talk later. But instead he said, "Look, y'all get started. I'll be right back."

"But we've already started," Charlotte called. "We need your input."

"Fine. I'll be right back."

Becca sped up, but not fast enough to outpace Nick and his long legs.

"Wait. Can we talk?"

"I'm at work, Nick. What's there to talk about?" She scanned the diner, and sure enough, every set of eyes were on them, including Zac's.

"I just want to make sure we're okay."

Becca grabbed another set of plates, the greasy smell coupled with the knot in her stomach making her feel queasy. "I told you yesterday that we were fine."

"Yet you just ran away from me like I was on fire. And then you were all weird yesterday, and I needed to talk to you." He lowered his voice and moved closer when Becca took a step back.

"Why don't you talk to your lawyer-doctor girlfriend?'

"My what?"

"Look, I'm busy and everyone's staring. Please just sit down and eat with the trustees before they break their necks trying to watch us argue. We'll talk later."

"But, Bec, I don't—"

"Later. Please."

She walked away before he could say another word, and Nick frowned as he took a seat at the end of the trustees' table. Then, realizing she had to take his order, she stopped beside him.

"Order."

"You know my order."

The trustees were all staring, but Becca couldn't keep her mouth shut another second. "Maybe I don't. There seems to be a lot about you you're not telling me these days. Seems I don't really know you at all."

"What is this about? You know me."

"Do I?"

"Becca, order up!"

Frustrated, Becca stomped her foot and shook her head and cursed under her breath like a person possessed by a demon. And hell if she wasn't possessed by a demon—the demon of want for Nick Hamilton. Eternal bachelor, his heart tied to a dead woman, and though Becca could respect that and would never want him to forget Britt, she was there, too. She'd been there all along. But no, he didn't want in her pants; he wanted in the doctor's pants.

"Waffle and eggs over easy."

"Fine."

"Fine," Nick replied.

"That's what I said, isn't it?"

Nick stood then and followed her. "What is your problem?"

"You."

Now not only was everyone staring but the entire diner had gone quiet, eager to hear every juicy word of the exchange. Fantastic. Becca had told herself that morning not to involve the town in her and Nick's mess, yet here they were, in front of the trustees no less, hashing it out.

"We are talking outside right now."

"No. We're not."

Nick's face creased with anger. "Fine, have it your way. If you won't talk out there, then we'll talk in here. You think I care what they think?" He waved around the diner, and Becca felt her cheeks burning bright from anger and embarrassment, each fighting it out for control. Damn him for acting like this! Damn him for making her care so much!

"Stop it."

"Not until you tell me what the hell is wrong with you."

"I told you. You. You're what's wrong."

"Me? What did I do?"

Becca's head was shaking so hard it might snap off any second, but she couldn't rein in her emotions any longer. "You get some fancy doctor girlfriend and you don't even tell me. I'm your best friend and you don't even tell me. And then—"

"Wait." Nick threw up a hand. "I what?"

"I can't talk about this right now."

"What's going on?"

They both looked over to see Trip standing in the doorway, watching them. "Y'all okay?"

"We're fine," Becca said, glaring at her best friend. "Perfectly fine. Nick was just taking his seat."

Nick swung at the incoming pitch, missing completely, and then swung again at the next pitch, only to miss again. What the hell? Were his glasses not doing their job all of a sudden?

He had found himself at the batting cages after the debacle at the diner, and even after an hour there, rain threatening to pour down on him, he still had no idea what was happening with Becca. And despite all the craziness at the office, his issues with his brothers, and the indecision weighing on him about the company, what bothered him the most was Becca being upset with him.

They'd been friends a long time, and though they were human and had the occasional fight, it was rare, and never like this. He felt sure he'd said something horrible to piss her off, but he couldn't figure out what. How could he apologize if he had no idea what to apologize for?

He swung again, eager to work off his pent-up aggravation, and made contact, only to watch the ball hit the chains at the top of the cage, soar back down, and smack him in the face.

"Ow." He yanked off his glasses and with now blurry vision examined them to find, sure enough, both lenses were cracked. "Freaking fantastic."

"You're having a time, aren't you?"

Nick tossed his glasses into a nearby trashcan and went back to swinging, ignoring Alex. "What are you doing here?"

"We came—"

"We?" Nick glanced around to see a fuzzy Trip standing beside Alex. "Perfect."

"We wanted to talk to you. Trip told me about what happened at the diner. You never fight with Becca, and you just had it out in the middle of the diner. We think Dad's death has hit you hard and you're refusing to address it. Now we're talking about selling Industries and you're holding on for him. Even if you know deep down it's a good decision to sell."

"What would you know about Industries? Either of you? You've stepped foot in that office what five times in your lives. I handle Industries."

"Is that what this is about?" Trip asked. "You want to be the one to decide? Fine. Decide. But don't let the business tank before you're willing to sell. Look at the numbers, man; they speak for themselves. We've peaked in the last few months, but sales are down for the year. Please, think about what you're doing. With the business. With us. And with Becca."

Nick paused, then got back into position, swung again, and missed.

"And your form is shit," Alex said, resulting in a sharp shove from Trip.

"Hey, don't piss him off any more than he already is. First Becca went off on him, now this."

"You don't know a thing about Becca and me."

Trip stepped inside the cages and set down a folder, then took a step back. "I know a lot more than you give me credit for. About Industries. And about you and Becca. I know you care for her, and I know you've been putting off telling her. Maybe you're scared. Maybe you think she won't share your feelings. But you more than anyone should know our days are numbered and we're not guaranteed anything. She deserves to know how you feel."

Nick eyed the folder, then his brother, the first hint of defeat working through him. He swallowed, delaying. "What if I'm not sure how I feel?"

"Then figure that out first. But once you know, tell her. She's amazing and she loves you."

"I don't know . . ."

"She loves you. We all know it. And we think you love her, too."

Nick stared at his brothers, unsure whether he could admit to loving her or even if he truly felt it. He knew Becca meant the world to him, but how could he go down that road again? He'd lost everyone who meant anything to him. What idiot walked into that hell for a fourth time?

He needed to think, and as much as it hurt, he needed to do it without Becca Stark.

Chapter Seven

One week. Okay, not a complete week, more like six days, but still. It had been six whole days since Becca had talked to Nick and she felt like an addict going through withdrawal. She had the shakes and her fingers kept twitching, like if left to their own devices they would find her cell phone and dial Nick and demand that he come over just so she could look at him and breathe and remind herself that her world hadn't changed.

She just wasn't talking to Nick.

And why? Because he had a doctor girlfriend and refused to tell her? Or was this because he'd said he didn't want to get into her pants, because who the hell got mad at that sort of thing? She should be pleased. She should be glad that she was friends with a guy who valued her friendship. But why *didn't* he want to get in her pants? Was she really that gross?

Surely not, right? Zac didn't seem to think so, but then, maybe something was inherently wrong with Zac. Like maybe he was blind to female grossness the way some men were color-blind.

No, Zac was too hot for that nonsense, so then what?

She reached for the tiny slip of paper on her kitchen counter, Zac's number written in perfectly legible ink. She should call him. She wanted to call him, but right now her brain could only handle the one complication, and until she fixed things with Nick, she couldn't do or think about anything else.

And what sucked the most was that in less than an hour she would be forced to see both of them. Assuming Nick showed, but what if he didn't?

As if on cue, her cell buzzed in her hand. She hadn't even realized she'd picked it up, but instead of Nick's name flashing across the screen, it was her mom.

"Hey, Mama," she said, answering.

"Your sister tells me that you gave her money. Again."

Becca walked around the island in her kitchen and opened the cabinet beside her refrigerator. She reached for her bottle of multivitamins, grabbed two; then, before shutting the cabinet, she eyed the bottle of mood positive. It was a vitamin B supervitamin, or maybe it had some voodoo to it, but regardless it worked, and clearly if Becca hoped to handle this conversation she would need an extra vitamin. Or twelve. Or maybe she should skip the vitamins and go straight for the hard stuff.

Chocolate.

"I had no choice, Mama. Ty lost his job again and the kids wanted cereal and she had no milk. What was I supposed to do?"

Her mother sighed into the phone. "She's never going to learn to walk if you keep carrying her."

Becca shook her head, though her mother couldn't see her, and slipped on her flip-flops to get ready to leave. Her mother loved to voice opinions from Florida, but if she were in Triple Run, she'd do the very same thing as Becca. They were too much alike, Becca her mother made over, which was maybe why her mother called her so often to give her grief. She'd spent years doing the very same thing for her own sister—bailing her out of bad marriage after bad marriage, and still Aunt Lydia hadn't learned a thing. Reagan would be the same way, yet Becca couldn't say no.

"She's family, Mama. I can't turn her away. And neither would you."

"Maybe not, but I'd make her work a little harder for it. You cave every time."

Becca grabbed her bag and walked out the door, not bothering to lock up. If a burglar wanted to steal her ancient TV, then so be it. Maybe he could figure out how to get it to switch channels. Presently, she had two options—a cooking show or the news, and Becca hated cooking.

"That's because she brings the kids with her every single time. I won't say no to them."

"She's going to bankrupt you."

Finally the weather was starting to feel like fall, a bit of a breeze in the air, and it reminded Becca of the first time Nick had arrived in her backyard. He'd gotten lost chasing after Trip, but he wouldn't admit it, so instead he acted like he was there to see her. Becca didn't really know him, but at eight years old, it thrilled her all the same for a boy to be there for her. So she asked him to come play dolls with her and he blanched and asked if they could play tag instead.

That was the start of Becca chasing Nick Hamilton. She'd never caught him then and she suspected she never would now.

"Sorry, Mama. Can we talk about this later? I'm heading out."

She could almost hear her mother's grin. "A date?"

Becca laughed. "I wish. But a man left me his number earlier this week at the diner."

"What does he do?"

"I don't know, Mama. Stuff."

"Hmmm . . ."

"I know what that sound means."

"Well. So what if I want the best for my little girl? You know who I think you should be with."

And Becca did. The very same man Becca wanted to be with, but all her and her mother's hope wouldn't make Nick Hamilton want her back.

"All right, talk later?" Becca needed off the call fast before the conversation headed any farther south.

"Okay, honey. Love you."

"Love you, too, Mama."

Becca hung up and took her time driving out to Crestler's Key for the dive lesson. Her thoughts turned inward and she wondered if her life was enough for her. She had money, owned her house, had a stable job. Surely those things equaled happiness, yet she couldn't remember feeling this miserable. Maybe it was time for a change, and not just repainting her house or buying distressed jeans instead of the dark ones she preferred.

Maybe it was time she left Triple Run.

The thought sliced straight through her heart, hanging over her like a dark cloud the whole ride over. Before long she reached Crestler's Key Elementary and parked, telling herself she didn't have to make that decision today. Her nerves twisted into minipretzels as she thought about the confrontations she was about to face. *Deep breath,* she told herself. *They're just boys. It's simple.*

Only they weren't boys and nothing about this was simple.

Resigned to stop being such a chicken, she closed the door to her Highlander and headed into the school, ignoring everything around her for fear that if she spotted an exit she would be far too tempted to take it.

Like always, the halls were empty and eerily quiet, so different from what they sounded like during the school week. Becca imagined walking down halls like these with her son or daughter, a smile on her face, tears in her eyes as she prepared to drop the boy or girl off for the first day of kindergarten. But would that ever happen for her?

No, not if she stayed hung up on Nick and not if she stayed in Triple Run.

You don't have to decide today.

The classroom neared and her heart kicked up. *Breathe, Becca. Breathe.* She closed her eyes and pushed through the door.

"Becca, hey there," Zac said. "Glad you're back for day two."

Becca smiled up at him, thankful that he wasn't making it awkward that she hadn't called him yet. "Thanks. I'm excited." Her gaze cut over to the class and landed square on Nick in the front row.

"Bec."

"Nick."

Torn over how to talk to him after their last conversation, she took the seat beside him and reached for her phone, as though she'd just gotten a call, then stuffed it back into her bag when she realized no one called her except her mother, who she'd already spoken to, and Nick, who apparently wasn't talking to her. Or maybe she wasn't speaking to him.

They fell into silence, the rest of the class chatting away, and Becca couldn't take it anymore. "Why aren't you talking to me?"

Nick glanced around. "Me?"

"No, the janitor outside mopping the floor. Yes, you."

"I'm not *not* talking to you. I thought you were upset with me."

"I am."

"You are or you were?"

Before Becca could reply, Zac took to the front of the class to start the lesson.

"Today we're taking a field trip to Southern Dive to try on equipment. So let's pack up. It's walking distance."

They started outside and Nick reached for Becca to stop her just as Zac stepped up beside them.

"So, I have to ask. Did you get my note?"

Becca grinned. "I did."

"Ah. So not interested?"

"It's not that. I just had a busy week."

Zac bit his lip and peered over at her. "All right. No pressure. But the offer's open whenever you'd like to take it."

"Thanks."

Zac disappeared up the sidewalk and into Southern Dive, and Nick reached for Becca to hold her back. "What was that about?"

She fidgeted with the zipper on her bag. "Nothing, really. He just gave me his number."

"Of course he did."

Anger surged through Becca. "See that? What is that? Why do you care?"

"I don't care. I just don't know why you didn't tell me."

Becca balled her hands into fists. "You're one to talk. You don't speak to me all week. And you kept your doctor girlfriend from me."

"Again with that. What the hell are you talking about?"

"Don't even deny it. First Kate and Alex all talking about you need to tell me and she's the one. And then Trip and Emery joke that only one woman has your attention these days. And then the trustees talk about your attention being on her."

Nick broke into laughter, and Becca thought she might scream.

"It isn't funny."

"No, you're right, it's freaking hilarious. You're ridiculous, you know that? Absolutely ridiculous."

"Because I don't want to be the last person to hear you're with someone now?"

Nick threw up his hands in frustration. "I'm not *with* someone now."

"Then what—"

"They're talking about you!"

Becca jerked back. "What?"

"They're all talking about you. When the hell would I have time to meet a woman, let alone a girlfriend? I spend every waking moment that I'm not at the office with you. They're talking about you."

"But you said . . ."

"I know what I said. I lied."

Nick stared at his best friend, wishing he could read her mind. Her expression was blank, giving nothing away, and he thought maybe he'd just made the worst decision of his life. And all because he was too jealous to control his emotions and his stupid mouth.

"I'm sorry, I . . ."

"I don't know what that means. Like are you saying . . ." Becca trailed off, because apparently neither of them could speak clearly now.

"I . . ." But before Nick could finish his thought, Zac popped out of Southern Dive's doorway.

"You two coming in? We need to select your equipment so we can plan to practice in the water next Saturday." His eyes drifted between the two of them before holding on Becca, and Nick felt his pulse picking up speed again, jealousy taking over, which was ridiculous. He'd never been the jealous sort, even with Britt, yet the idea of another man's hands on Becca sent his head into crazy territory.

Becca eyed Nick. "Yeah, we're coming right now."

They stepped inside Southern Dive, and if not for the tension between him and Becca, he would have been in heaven. The shop had everything one could imagine related to diving.

Stained-wood walls and wide hardwood floors gave the place a rustic feel. Large brand signs hung against the back wall, mixed with enlarged photos of dives the Littleton brothers had been on over the years. Some were of class dives, but others were just them, exploring some abandoned shipwreck or on an exotic underwater adventure.

The class had already spread out through the shop, some trying on BCDs, others masks, still others the various types of wet suits. And Becca was right there with them, each piece of equipment seeming to take longer than the last, and before long Nick wondered if Becca was intentionally dragging it out so she wouldn't have to talk to him.

Finally, when she'd tried on no less than twenty different wet suits, he tossed up his hands, unable to handle the tension any longer. "Look, Bec, I'm going to head out."

"But you haven't selected anything."

"I already have all these things, and I . . . I just can't stay here anymore, doing this."

"I know it's a little boring choosing equipment, but—"

"Not that. This; you and me. Whatever this weirdness is between us. We need to talk about it."

Becca refused to look at him. "I don't . . . it . . ." Her eyes finally met his. "I can't right now."

Nick stared at her wide brown eyes, her mouth set into a frown, the class around them, half of them staring, and he'd had enough.

"I have to go."

"Don't leave."

He took in her face, the quick glance to Zac, and knew he'd made a terrible mistake. "I'll see you around, Bec."

Part of him wanted her to follow after him, to tell him that she felt the same way, but another part of him wanted to avoid the topic so they could pretend it had never come up.

Telling himself that for now they needed space to think, he hopped into his car with the sole purpose of driving until he knew what to do. Though he feared revelation would never come. This wasn't some complex project to which deep thought and planning would reveal answers. Feelings weren't so easy to process, especially when those feelings shouldn't exist in the first place.

It shouldn't have surprised Nick that he ended up on the long, winding road that led into the heart of Hamilton Stables. Though he spent more time at his apartment in Lexington, he still viewed the farm as his home. He might be at odds with his brothers, but they were still family, and maybe the only people in the world who could talk him off the ledge.

Because what Nick really wanted to do was go wait at Becca's house until she came home, force her to talk, to answer the question plaguing him—*Do you want me as badly as I want you?* But he feared he wouldn't find a friend who'd always thought about him the way he'd thought of her, just an awkward silence in place of an answer. A sad look and an "I'm sorry" and Nick would lose her.

God, why the hell had he confessed his feelings?

So what if his brothers and the town thought he had feelings for her; that didn't mean anything, or at least it didn't have to. He could have denied it, made up something else, tucked away his desires for a safer time. But in that moment, her beautiful face before him, those soulful eyes of hers trained on him, he couldn't hide his reaction. Now he might have ruined the only friendship he had left.

"Long time no see," Mama V said as he parked beside the main barn.

As usual, the grounds were impeccable, all green and vibrant. The woods surrounding the farm full and beautiful. The white fencing had been painted recently and the main offices and barns renovated for the upcoming tour season. As Nick took in all the beauty of the farm where he was raised, he found himself wondering why he didn't join the farm instead of Industries. Why he didn't find a place here with his brothers instead of going out on his own with Industries? His father could have hired someone to run Industries when he retired, he could have promoted someone; there were a thousand options available.

Instead, Nick dove headfirst into Industries, when on the farm he would have been free of the stress of corporate life. Every day he could have stepped outside to fresh air and visited the horses, breathed a little.

But no, he chose the other path before him, never stopping to think whether he actually wanted to be a corporate man.

He thought of his high school dream of being a pro angler, how close he'd been, and then the decision to go to Northwestern, his father's idea; a degree could only help him.

He'd met Britt his sophomore year and was immediately captivated by her. She was earthy in a worn book kind of way, an English lit major, with aspirations to seek her MFA and become a distinguished literary novelist/professor. And she was well on her way when tragedy struck.

She went in for her annual women's checkup, and that was how they first found the lump in her breast. At first, no one was overly worried. She was healthy; tired but healthy. And then her blood work came back before she'd had the chance to get in for her CT scan, and suddenly everything was urgent.

The CT showed stage III breast cancer. She had more tumors hiding within her breasts that weren't so easily detected by a breast exam. She was referred to an oncologist and her first surgery was scheduled, and they were hopeful. God, they were hopeful.

But then chemo and radiation, and more chemo and radiation, only to go back in to find the cancer still there, living despite all the chemicals they threw at it.

Nick would never forget the look on her doctor's face when she told Britt they'd done all they could do. He was holding her when she took her last breath, and still to this day, he would wake sometimes and feel like he was back there, holding her, knowing any second would be his last with her and desperate to hold on just a few seconds longer.

He didn't think he would survive her death, and in some ways he didn't. The Nick he'd been before died along with her.

But now, so many years later, he wondered not if he'd ever loved her, because he knew he had, but if she was ever the right wife for him—the true love of his life. Though the thought made him feel sick to his core, he couldn't deny the validity of the question.

She'd never fished with him, never taken a picture of him after a giant catch, and there was no way she ever would have done something as radical as learning to scuba dive.

Britt was the very opposite of Becca, and yet at the time she'd seemed like the perfect match for him. She was Ivy League, from a solid family, had Southern roots in Alabama, with her mother's grandparents. And Nick's mother adored her immediately, though it was hard not to. Britt was polite to a fault, forever smiling, never loud or inappropriate. But that also meant she was never wild, never free-spirited, never adventurous. Which was fine. One didn't have to be adventurous, but the problem was—Nick was.

At heart, at root, in his joints and bones and muscles, he craved T-shirts rather than pressed button downs, wet suits rather than business suits. It surprised him to think about it, but his years of diving with his brothers out in the Gulf, in Fiji, hundreds of different dives, had been some of the best memories of his life.

But there was a woman who thrived on those same things, who may never be athletic but craved the wind against her face all the same. How had he not seen that before?

Nick had a perfect match and she'd been there all along. From the awkward little girl to the sassy teen to a woman who put her life on hold to take care of her grandmother. He had a match and her name was Becca Stark.

"Honey, are you all right?"

Nick glanced past Mama V to the main barn, then the training ring nearby. "Is Trip around?"

"He's at the track."

"Alex?"

"Visiting Trifecta Farms to pick up that new stallion."

"Dammit." Nick released a breath. "What now?"

"Why don't you come inside for a beat?" Mama V said, motioning to her house on the farm, where she kept her kitchen running and open for the farm's staff.

Nick hesitated. He never talked about his feelings, and he had a strict rule never to reveal too much of himself to the staff. What might they think if he showed all his weaknesses? But Mama V was different. She'd been around since he was little, was best friends with his mother, knew him on that deeper level that came from watching a boy become a man.

"Come on. Let me mother you a little."

With reluctance, he stepped through the door directly into the kitchen, the smell of bread baking hitting his nose. "You know, Mama V, you could give Patty and Annie-Jean a run for their money."

The old woman winked. "Why don't you ask Patty who taught her how to bake sometime?"

That had Nick laughing. Patty acted as though she'd invented the Bundt cake and would freeze you with her glare if you tried to suggest otherwise. "Really, now? I had no idea. She'd be angry if she heard you telling people that."

Mama V waved the comment off as ridiculous. "Patty's parents used to live beside me and Earl years ago. She used to pop in every day after school and I'd teach her a thing or two. Before long, she went from making mud pies to real pies. The rest is history, I guess."

"Wow, V, you really are a legend around Triple Run."

The old woman smiled. "I do my best, but we aren't here to talk about me." She set down a plate with a slice of banana nut bread on it and placed a cup of black coffee beside it. Nick took a long sip, thankful he'd stopped by, or else he was liable to do something really stupid, like call Becca and scream that he loved her, why couldn't she just love him back?

"What's troubling you, son? Is this about a girl?"

Nick's gaze snapped over. "How did you . . . ?"

Her grin spread. "Whenever a man looks dumbfounded, I know it involves a woman."

"Well . . . it's . . . see it's . . ." He trailed off, unsure exactly where to begin. Then he remembered that Mama V knew Becca, had watched her grow up with the boys around the farm. "You know Becca Stark?"

"Honey, everybody knows Becca. No one could forget a face like that, plus her smile? It'd lighten the darkest night." *Wasn't that the damn truth?* "But something tells me you know that."

"I made a mistake. We've been friends forever, and I adore her. I need her. She's my best friend. After Dad died, I had no one. Only Becca, and now . . ."

She tossed up a finger to stop him. "Well, now, that's not true. Your brothers are your blood. They love you. And this farm loves you. This is your home."

Nick stared out the kitchen windows to the staff walking by, to the ones working horses on the grounds. She was right. Most of these people had been with them for years, for much of Nick's life.

"But just because you have other people doesn't mean those people can fill the void. Becca fills your void."

Swallowing hard, Nick peered back over at Mama V. "Like no one else ever has."

"Then tell her. She loves you, too, boy. Surely you see that."

"She didn't say anything."

"When you told her you loved her?"

Nick paused, rethinking the conversation. "I didn't actually tell her that."

"Then what did you say?"

Suddenly, Nick stood up. "Nothing. I told her others suspected we were together, that I cared for her."

"But you didn't confirm it?"

Nick ran through the conversation again. He hadn't told her a damn thing. Was that why she'd frozen up? Because he'd said all those things without confirming them? He didn't know, but it was time he found out.

"Where are you going?" Mama V called as he started for the door.

He winked back at her. "To see about a girl."

Chapter Eight

Becca decided that Carrie Underwood sang songs especially for her, because right that second she totally needed a "Smoke Break," though she'd never smoked a day in her life, and to be "Blown Away" so she no longer had to feel any more . . . or see anyone in town who could remind her of all the things she'd never have.

Her heart hurt in a way she'd never experienced before. The closest was when Nick had come home that summer before his junior year, Britt beside him, and that goofy grin on his face that said he was in love. Only it wasn't directed at her, like she'd always dreamed. She'd put on makeup and fixed her hair and tried her best to look like a girl Nick would want, and the realization that she wasn't that girl had been devastating. His smile wasn't for her. It was for another girl, and that was the day she'd had a heart-to-heart with herself about Nick Hamilton. He would never be hers, never see her as more.

And today did nothing more than confirm that harsh reality.

She took another long sip of her beer, because she still had it in her fridge from when Nick was there last, and though she hated the taste of the stuff, she needed something to keep from falling over the edge into depression oblivion.

Because she was close. Closer than she'd ever been in her life. Even when her grandmother died and her heart was broken, she knew she had others around to support her and help her deal with the pain. Nick was around. But with him being the reason for her heartache, she had no one to turn to.

The thought of Nick being with a doctor girlfriend had been a tough pill to swallow, but then he'd told her that there wasn't a girlfriend and they'd been talking about her, and for a moment her heart had soared. Finally, finally, he was seeing her. He had realized what she'd realized in that first game of tag—they were meant to be to-gether.

But then he'd just stared at her, with her staring back, never con-firming that what they said meant anything at all, and she knew why—to him it was a giant joke. Nick falling for Becca; oh, how hilarious.

She took another long pull of her beer and grimaced, kicking her feet against her back porch so the swing she'd collapsed into would move, her arm draped over her eyes so she wouldn't have to look at the sun bragging about how big and bright it was. Becca was a mess, a giant, humiliated mess. Carrie Underwood should sing a song about her life. It'd sell a million copies, and people would sing and sing about how pitiful it was to love a man who would never love you back.

Dear God, she was now comparing her life to sad country songs.

Another sip of beer had her grimacing, and she tried to set the beer down on the porch without looking up at the arrogant sun and narrowly kept from falling out of the swing.

"Give me that before you fall on your face. Besides, you hate beer."

Becca lifted her arm to peer at the man leaning against the railing on her porch, his arms crossed over his chest. He wore a Hamilton Stables T-shirt and worn jeans, reminding Becca of the boy she'd once known. Long before the Ivy League education and three-thousand-dollar suits, long before the fiancée and the deaths that had all but de-stroyed him.

"What are you doing here?"

"I had something important to tell you."

"Okay?"

"I want you."

The beer bottle slipped from her grasp and she tried to grab it, but agile Becca was not, so the bottle shattered into a thousand pieces on her porch. "Crap."

"See."

She glanced up, her heartbeat picking up speed. "What did you just say?"

"I said 'see.' "

"No, before that."

Nick smiled at her, the picture of ease as he took a step toward her, then two. "I said I want you. I wanted you at eight. I wanted you at eighteen. And I want you now. That part has never been in question. Doubt whatever you want, but don't doubt that. I want you. Trip and Alex, the town, they all think you're my match because I can't stop talking about you, can't even look at anyone else. For me, there's only ever been you."

"But what about our friendship?"

Nick edged one step closer, but the impact on her heart had the weight of a thousand. It felt like they'd been walking toward each other for a lifetime, only to finally find the right route.

Tentatively, he reached out, his gaze trained on her hand as he linked his fingers through hers. Like something miraculous was happening, and maybe, just maybe, it was. "I don't know." Then he flicked his eyes up to meet hers. "But if I don't do this, I'm going to go insane."

And then in one more move he had her in his arms, his face coming down to meet hers as he captured her lips with his, a soft groan escaping him as though he finally had the one thing he'd always craved. He cradled her face in his large hands and beckoned her lips to part, his tongue slipping inside, commanding her into his world, all control lost. All thought gone, all worry dispelled as their bodies melded together. Becca pushed herself closer and closer to him, terrified that if she let go he would leave. The dream would be over.

Finally, Nick pulled away, his breath heavy, his eyes dark with emotion and need. "That was . . . I . . ." And then, instead of continuing, he leaned in again, the sweet kiss from before turning even more intense. He pecked her lips once more before struggling to pull away. "I've dreamed of doing that for years, but I had no idea it would be like that."

Becca tried to take a step back so she could think, but he secured her to him. "Na-ah. I've just gotten you. I don't want to let you go."

"But see, that's just it. You haven't just gotten me. You've always had me." Becca bit her lip. "And I'm not sure my heart could take the letdown if this ends and our friendship is ruined."

Hints of night sounded all around them—crickets playing their melody, leaves rustling in the gentle breeze. The moment drew on, before Nick finally took his own step back, his hands on his hips. "What do we do? I don't want to ruin it either, but I want this. Good God, do I ever want this."

"Enough to risk our friendship?"

When Nick's face fell, she had her answer. He started to say something when she waved him off. "It's okay."

"No. Nothing about this is okay. Why does it have to be all or nothing? Can we try to still be friends if it doesn't work? Though with a kiss like that, how could it not work?"

Becca laughed, and he took her hand, pressing a soft kiss to it before linking his fingers through hers. "Can we at least think about it?"

"Yes, let's think about it. Thinking sounds good."

"But for today, can we go back to kissing?"

Another laugh escaped her. "How about we go out to dinner instead? A safe zone."

"You should know that I'll just be thinking about kissing you."

Becca leaned in and easily kissed his lips once more, unable to stay away.

"I hope so."

Nick pulled into Balls, Clowns, and Other Fun Stuff, the only miniature golf place in the area. It was located smack between Triple Run and Crestler's Key, so Chester Young, the owner, wouldn't have to claim to be in one town or the other and could garner business from both towns.

The name was as tacky as the putt-putt site itself, and most of the mothers around town refused to bring their kids there on principle alone. So the place was far more likely to be filled with teens and adults than children, and very few from Triple Run.

The whole place bordered on the inappropriate, and the clowns were reminiscent of that freakish one in the movie *It*. Yet, as Nick parked and smiled over at Becca, he knew this was the very place they needed to be. Away from the regular crowd and the gossip that surrounded them there, a beautiful twinkling night sky above them, and enough people around to keep them on the good side.

If in action alone.

"Putt-putt golf." Becca shut the car door and started toward the entrance, then stopped and cocked her head. "Wow, that's . . . something else."

Nick's smile took over his face as he fought to rein in his laughter. To enter the putt-putt area, you had to walk through two giant clowns high-fiving each other, while their other hands were coyly covering their mouths, their eyes glancing away. "You realize this place makes the trustees' list of businesses to ban every single month."

Nick laughed. "Yeah, but you gotta admit Chester had balls to build a place like this, and it's never dead here. He makes a killing and nothing about it is too obvious."

"Yeah, but it's tasteless."

"Yep. And the very place we needed to hang out tonight. A little outside-the-norm fun. Besides, they sell popcorn, and you know you can never refuse that fake popcorn stuff."

A smile played at Becca's lips as she peered over at him, causing that heat in his stomach to rekindle to life. Now that they'd kissed, he ached to do it again, the need within him and the desire to feel her against him enough to make it impossible to be around her without touching her.

Yet he knew if he did, if he held her hand, he'd pull her to him, he'd press his lips to hers, eager to see if she made the small satisfied sounds every time he kissed her or if that was just part of the first-kiss wonder.

But still . . . those sounds, her lips, the thought of those long legs of hers wrapped around his waist as he—

"Nick? You coming?"

He'd stopped walking without realizing it.

"And why are you staring at me like that?"

His gaze lifted from the legs in question to her face. "You're beautiful, that's why. It's hard to be around you without staring."

The small smile crept across her face. "You're going to have to hide that charm if we're going to really think about this in the way we should."

"Fine. I'll hide my charm if you hide your legs, because right now I'm having terribly inappropriate visions of them, and I'd hate to have an accident or something because I'm unable to focus."

"You're such a flirt."

"Only with you."

Nick realized how true that statement was, though he'd said it to her a thousand times, and wondered how long he'd had a thing for Becca. He knew he'd always been attracted to her, but this felt like something different. Something more.

And that scared the shit out of him.

He cared for Becca, and damn if he didn't want to find out what sounds she'd make in bed, but could he really do the relationship thing again? Could he risk falling head over heels for her and then losing her? He wasn't sure he'd survive losing another person he loved.

But as they paid at the entrance, slap between the legs of the two clowns, Becca giggling up at them, he realized for now he didn't have to worry about it. And he didn't want to. For now, avoidance was the name of the game—with selling Industries and with worry over a commitment with Becca. Because Trip had been right about one thing: Nick had lost enough to realize the value of living in the moment. And he was ready to do just that.

"All right, it looks like Mr. Couldn't Wait on the Potty to Open Up is number one." Becca pointed to the first hole, and sure enough, there was a giant clown beside the hole spraying water from a flower in his hand, but with Chester's humor, the flower was positioned so that at first glance it looked like the clown was peeing across the green into the water running on the opposite side.

"Well, if a man's got to go, a man's got to go."

She grinned. "Reminds me of that time we got lost in the woods trying to find that field with the baby calf and I had to go to the bathroom, and you told me just to go and I told you I couldn't just go in the woods, and you said, 'sure you can, watch.' Then you walked around a tree and nodded like I should find my own tree."

"Hey! I was nine and clearly an idiot."

"No doubt there. But you were a cute idiot."

He brushed his shoulder against hers. "You were cute, too. Still are."

"No charm, remember?" She pointed at him as she swung her putter, missing the hole by an inch. "Dammit, so close."

Nick edged around her, trailing his hand around her as he moved, and leaned in, drawing in her summertime scent. "Very close indeed." She turned toward him, their faces a breath apart, and that was when he heard his name being shouted from the entrance.

They jumped apart, and he searched the entrance for the source of the shouting, to find Trip, Emery, Alex, and Kate all waving at them. And starting their way.

"Just my luck."

"Be nice," Becca said.

"I'm always nice."

"To me."

"You're the only one who matters."

Becca's gaze fell on his. "I don't know what to do when you say things like that. I mean, are these the kinds of things you've been thinking all along? And you're wrong. You're the nice Hamilton, always have been. Don't let whatever is going on between you and them keep you from being yourself. You're not a jerk."

"What if I want to be a jerk?"

"Too bad, you're not. And they're your family," Becca managed to add before the brothers were before them, and Nick's jaw ticked.

"Hey." With a quick glance at his brothers, Nick walked around Becca, focused on the hole, and knocked his ball in.

Trip started to ask something, when another shout had them all look up, and Nick groaned. Clearly, he'd chosen the worst place on the planet to be semialone with Becca.

"Charlie!" Kate rushed up to her brother, hugging him close. "When did you get back? I thought you were at that farmer's convention out west."

Charlie grinned down at his sister. "Made it back a few hours ago, and we decided to head here instead of to a bar."

"We?" Nick asked, and then his agitation spiked as Charlie's gaze fell on him and he smirked before flipping his attention to Nick's left.

"Becca! Good to see you again." He reached a hand over to her and she shook it. "Seems like I hear your name all the time." And that was when Zac and Brady appeared beside their brother, all three of them dressed in Southern Dive T-shirts and jeans, like some poster in a freaking magazine.

Nick's heated gaze drifted from Charlie to Zac, then finally to Becca. "I didn't realize you were all so close."

"We've been by the diner a few times. Hard to miss a face like Becca's."

At that Nick stiffened, and Trip and Alex stepped up beside him, sensing his unease and sizing up the Littleton brothers. "Is there a problem we don't know about?" Trip asked, always the big brother.

"No problem," Zac replied, flexing as he crossed his arms over his chest, equally all big brother.

"What the hell is happening?" Becca muttered, but Nick couldn't explain this to her. He could scarcely explain it to himself. But the words *pissing match* were rolling around in his mind, though he'd never considered himself an overly competitive man. Clearly, Becca brought out his competitive side, along with a wealth of other emotions he wasn't prepared to handle.

Emery grinned at Nick, the definition of an annoying big sister, though she wasn't blood, and then leaned in closer to Becca. "I think the Hamilton and the Littleton brothers are fighting it out for you. Like which family you belong to."

"What? I don't belong to either of them."

"They seem to think you do." Kate stood beside the other two women, smiling, and Nick wanted to stop this, tell them all they were acting like asses, but then he caught Zac checking Becca out, and suddenly he was crossing his arms, flexing his biceps.

Two could plan this game.

"Can we just play?" Becca asked, stepping in front of Nick, clearly hoping to help him see reason, but there was no reason to this, no logic anywhere in sight. All he could see was Zac and that grin of his, and then before he could help himself, he said, "How about a little competition? Us against you."

"Fine," Zac said. "But why don't we make this more interesting."

"What are you thinking?"

"A little wager?"

Alex laughed as he leaned against his brother. "You sure you want to bet against us? Might leave here a little embarrassed."

Charlie grinned back, but nothing about his smile was light. "We'll see."

"A hundred?"

Nick shrugged. "A hundred? You call that interesting? Why don't we make it five?"

"Fine by us," Brady said, propping an arm on Zac's shoulder. "Your funeral."

"Ladies, keep score?" Trip called, and Emery glared at him.

"Hell no. We're playing, too," Emery said. "Keep your own score."

And so the game began.

"Nick . . ." Becca started.

"It's just a little fun."

"It doesn't sound like fun. It sounds like you're throwing balls instead of fists."

At that he started laughing. "Trust me, it's fine." He walked over to her and kissed her forehead, earning confusion-filled stares from his brothers and huge grins from their wives. But he wasn't doing it for them, and when he caught Zac's glare, he knew that while he might not be the competitive sort, Zac clearly was. And he planned to win more than just the stupid putt-putt game. He intended to win Becca.

Even if he felt like a raging asshole for thinking it.

"Who's first?" Trip asked. "Flip for it?" He took a quarter from his pocket and eyed Zac. "Call it." He flipped the coin as Zac called tails and then it hit the ground, heads facing up, and the Hamilton brothers went crazy.

This was going to be the juiciest win of Nick's life.

The Hamiltons huddled together all serious-like, and for the first time in weeks, Nick felt like they were brothers again, family, that bond that was there before their father died returning as they unified to beat the Crestler's Key brothers.

Because what Becca and Emery and Kate didn't know was that this wasn't the first competition these sets of brothers had faced off against. They'd played each other growing up, their ages stair-stepping perfectly. Zac was Trip's age, Charlie was Nick's, and Brady was Alex's, so it was only natural that the Hamiltons would become Triple Run's golden boys and the Littletons would be Crestler's Key's favorites.

Of course, they'd split sports halfway down the middle, each of them involved in different ones, so that the Hamiltons owned baseball, with their tall, lean, muscular frames, and the Littletons owned football, with their more bulky, rustic frames.

As far as the farms went, there was no comparison. Hamilton Stables was expressly a horse farm, and the Littletons' Orchard Farm was a traditional fruit and vegetable one. With acres and acres of apple trees, Orchard Farm had become one of the most popular spots in the South during the fall for U-pick apple picking, corn mazes, and hay rides. They were family fun, where Hamilton Stables was all prestige.

And that was part of the animosity.

The Littletons had always viewed the Hamiltons as pretty boys who'd never lifted a finger in their lives. Forget that Trip single-handedly built Hamilton Stables and was a world-renowned horse trainer. Or that Alex had built the breeding division. Or that back in the day, Nick had had a shot at becoming a pro angler. None of that mattered. To the Littletons, they were white-collar rich boys. End of story.

Well, these rich boys were about to show those country boys up.

"Nick's the better golfer, but Alex is the better athlete," Trip said. "So Alex starts, then I'll go, and Nick can close us." They clapped to break, like they were on a football field, and then it was all glaring at the opponent and serious strategy talk while the women disappeared to the other course, annoyed at the men's antics.

"Beers all around?" Brady asked, and once the alcohol started flowing, it didn't stop.

Soon beer took over logic and reason, and the competition morphed into who could hit the ball out of the most difficult spot. On his turn, Alex edged into the water, claiming he could hit his ball out of there, that he still had a shot, while Kate screamed from across the course to get his ass out of the water. He was a man, not a child. And then both sets of brothers were laughing hysterically.

They finally reached the final hole, half a case of beers in each of them, and Nick was up. He had just decided that his glasses were broken, because his vision had blurred and his head buzzed, when he glanced up and caught sight of Becca at a hole above them. The wind caught her long locks so they flowed behind her, her face glowing in the warm light, and damn if he wasn't lost. Absolutely lost. All his goals, everything he'd told himself his entire life tied up in this decision, and he had no idea what to do.

"Got it bad, huh?" Zac said from behind him, and Nick peered over.

"Apparently. When the hell did that happen?"

Zac patted his shoulder. "A girl like that? Probably the moment you met her."

Nick's thoughts drifted back to when he first saw her in her backyard, and sure enough, he'd stopped walking, his jaw falling slack, all thought on this girl and how the hell he'd never noticed her before. Surely she didn't go to his school. But it turned out she did. He'd spent the better part of five years tripping all over her, for her never to notice, and then she'd called him her best friend and he just knew any hope was over, death by the friend card.

But now, looking at her, the most beautiful thing he'd ever seen, he wondered why he'd never thought to ask her for more back then. To try. How different his life might have been if he'd just tried.

"You're up, bro," Alex said. "Think you got it in you?"

Nick's gaze held on Becca. "I wish I knew."

It was the final putt for the Hamiltons, and then the Littletons would have an opportunity to tie it up and then there would have to be a putt off.

Nick hit the ball just as the clown's mouth opened up, and the ball disappeared inside, and then all the men raced over to the other side of the hole to see where the ball would end up. It bounced off wall after wall, before rolling slowly toward the hole.

"Come on, ball," Alex screamed, and even Trip had his hands clenched like he was praying. All eyes were on the ball, and then their breaths held as it rolled closer and closer and then—

"Yes!" Nick and his brothers all jumped at the same time as the ball dropped into the hole. "Hole in one. Beat that, Littletons!" All right, so maybe they were a little more than drunk now.

"We got this, don't you worry," Zac called, his voice slurring, and suddenly Nick found the whole competition to be the stupidest thing he'd ever done in his life.

"What are we doing here?" he asked.

Zac stared at him. "Playing putt-putt, dude. It's serious stuff."

"You know what? I don't think I hate you after all," Nick said, his turn to slur. "Damn, how much have we drunk?" He turned to ask one of his brothers, tripped over the clown's giant shoe, and toppled hands and knees into the bright blue stream cradling the hole. "Shit."

All the men burst out laughing, and Becca appeared in front of him, her hands on her hips.

"What did you get yourself into?"

His gaze lifted, and suddenly, the alcohol in his veins made it impossible for him to be anything other than truthful. "I don't want to screw us up, but I don't want anyone else. Only you, Bec. It's always been you."

Her own gaze drifted past him, likely to his brothers and their wives and the Littletons, all of them thinking he was some lovesick sap, and maybe he was. He'd been sad for so long that he wasn't sure how to breathe or work or be anymore, but then he'd be around Becca and everything would be all right again. His body would remember how to function, her bringing him back to neutral, and that sort of relief couldn't be ignored.

Finally, she reached down and helped Nick out of the water. "You're going to drench your car."

"I don't care."

"I know."

"Kiss me."

"Nick, we agreed to think about this."

"I have. I don't want to think anymore." He stepped closer and closer, until he stood inches from her, towering over her. "Kiss me."

"You're drunk."

He shrugged. "Maybe, but I've never seen things more clearly." He leaned in, his mouth hovering over hers, the smell of chlorine all over him, and yeah, maybe he was a little drunk and his family and God knew who else was watching, but he was ready. He had to be ready. "Kiss me."

And then his mouth grazed hers and all restraint was gone. He pulled her to him, the moon high above, and all he could think was—finally. Because this kiss wasn't rash, this wasn't a rush of hormones, this was all them, back to the beginning, slower moves and deeper feelings. His lips moved over hers like a caress, the pressure impossibly light, but force didn't seem right here. He didn't want to mess this up, to push too far, and he could feel her hesitation, sense it in her moves. But even she couldn't deny the chemistry between them.

Finally, he pulled away and pressed his forehead to hers. "I'll never grow tired of kissing you. Tell me we can give this a go."

"I don't know . . ."

"Do you trust me?" Nick stared down at her, ignoring the catcalls from his drunken brothers and the clown laughing beside him. Ignoring everything but this woman in his arms, in his heart.

She glanced up at him, her lips slightly parted, her cheeks flushed. "Yes."

"Then trust me now."

He caught the change in her eyes even before she spoke, and then he was kissing her again, this time with more eagerness.

Finally, everything in his life felt right. He and his brothers were talking again and the woman he'd loved all his life was beside him.

What could possibly go wrong?

Chapter Nine

"Order up, Bec," Sage called from the order counter.

Becca finished pouring the glass of tea in her hand, her thoughts clouded. The truth was they'd been clouded for the better part of a week now. She still couldn't believe she and Nick were together, though they'd never used any titles, so maybe they weren't exactly together but just dating. Like casual dating. Were they casual dating? And what did that mean exactly? Like could he date other people?

Oh, God, was he dating other people?

"Becca, you're going to need a rag if you don't stop pouring soon." She peered down at Charlotte's glass and sure enough, she'd filled it to the tippy top, narrowly missing overfilling it, thanks to Charlotte stopping her.

"I'm so sorry. Let me get you a straw so you can sip it down." She pulled a straw from her apron and passed it to Charlotte, who was sitting with a few of the other town trustees. No doubt yet another meeting about the festival that weekend.

Charlotte grinned up at her. "Don't you worry yourself, honey. We know you've had your hands full, keeping that last Hamilton happy."

Becca's gaze snapped from the straw to Charlotte's face. "I'm sorry?" Did sixty-two-year-old Charlotte really just say what Becca thought she'd said?

"Nick. It's all over town that you've scooped him up for yourself."

Janice Valks leaned around Mayor Phillips. "Such a Cinderella story, too. Everyone's talking about a spring wedding."

At that, Becca dropped the other straws she'd been holding. "No, no. No spring wedding."

"But whyever not?" Janice asked, her gray eyebrows knitting together. She dressed in a different matching velour outfit every day, and today she wore red. Her gray hair had long since been cut short. "A wealthy man like that and a poor girl like you? It'll make a fantastic story for the *Tribune*, and then you can quit the diner. Make a better life for yourself. Don't you want a better life for yourself?"

Becca wasn't sure if she should be shocked or offended or both. "Nick and I are . . ." She started to say friends, the explanation she'd given for years, but that title didn't work for them anymore. Friends didn't kiss the way they kissed, and Lord above, could that man kiss. Her knees went a little weak thinking about it, until Mayor Phillips said, "A wedding in Town Square would be a lovely affair."

"Y'all, we're not getting married."

Charlotte's eyebrows lifted and she shook her head. "Well, you'd better close the deal soon. A fine man like that will not be on the market forever, and what better options do you have, dear? He's a Hamilton. You're a Stark. This is your Jane Austen moment, your Cinderella moment. Don't let it pass you by."

What better options did she have? Was that really what the town thought of her? That she was no better than a waitress, not worthy of Nick?

And then it hit her—maybe they were right. How could she compete against all those upper-class women he met at work and around the farm? Horse racing was a very prestigious sport, and there was no shortage of beautiful women vying for the attention of the Hamiltons.

Becca could never compete against them in her current state, apron greasy from the French fries splattering on her earlier and her hair in a messy bun on the top of her head. She wore not a stitch of makeup because it would just melt off by the end of her shift, which all led to one hard truth—she wasn't Hamilton material. She needed to do something more, seek out something that would launch her up the social ladder. But with a name like Stark and a town like Triple Run, was that even possible?

Just then her gaze caught on a flyer on the diner's window. She cocked her head to try to read the words with the flyer facing in the opposite direction. Recruiter. Oh my God, recruiter! She'd completely forgotten about Priscilla!

With new determination, she pulled off her apron and set it behind the counter. "I'll be right back."

"Wait, where are you going?" Sage called as she started for the door. "We've got a full house."

"Willow's here. She can handle it for fifteen minutes."

"It's not your lunch yet," the cook argued.

Becca eyed the pack of cigarettes in his shirt pocket. "Consider this my smoke break."

"But you don't smoke."

"Yeah, well, maybe sometimes I need a smoke break, too. I'll be back in fifteen." And then Becca disappeared outside before he could continue the argument, growing more frustrated with each step. So what if she didn't smoke? Why should smokers get all the breaks? They shouldn't. Nonsmokers deserved smoke breaks, too, and she was taking hers. Sage could fire her if he wanted.

Of course, the diner *was* in the middle of the lunch rush, so he might do just that for her walking out, but she couldn't stand there another second without a solid plan in mind. And no one in this town could help her get a plan in place better than Priscilla.

She drew a breath and released it. The afternoon fall air was light, easy to breathe, the leaves changing from the green of summer to the beautiful reds and oranges that made Becca love the season so much.

With a quick glance both ways, Becca cut across Town Square to Rosaline Street, the home of most of the local businesses, all of them in old homes converted into shops or hair salons or small businesses, yet their outsides still looked like something out of an old television show.

Passing Doc Easton's Family Practice and then Country Interiors and Landscaping, Becca walked up the long sidewalk to Triple Run Recruiting, the only job-hunting place in town. Though she thought Priscilla's job might be better described as sitting in her office and pretending to look for jobs for others, while she really researched town gossip.

Regardless, Becca was desperate. She needed a true career, something that didn't involve carrying pitchers of sweet tea.

"Hey, honey," Priscilla said as soon as Becca walked through the door. "I saw you marching down the sidewalk. Did Sage piss you off again?"

Becca took in the woman, all curled white-blonde hair and overly made up face, pearls around her neck, a classy blouse and black trousers completing the look. She was one of the few people in town who hadn't grown up here, instead settling here after living up north and out west and even in Florida for a while. At first, the town had refused to accept her out of principle alone, their eyebrows cocked as she opened Triple Run Recruiting, but then someone would need a job and they'd stumble in there, and Priscilla would find them something. Suddenly, her worth outweighed her lack of heritage.

"I need a job."

"Did Sage fire you?"

"No." *Though he might after this*, Becca thought.

"Then why do you need a job?" Priscilla placed a manicured hand on her hip and stared at Becca. Even Priscilla looked more put together than Becca. Maybe she should marry Nick, though of course she was old enough to be his mother, so that might pose a little problem for him.

"I'm not doing anything with my life. Being anything. I want to be something. Have a title by my name that garners respect."

Priscilla opened her mouth, then closed it back and peered at the waitress. "Come on in. Let's chat about who Becca Stark is."

They walked into Priscilla's office, the decor all cherry wood against deep tans and grays—very modern yet sophisticated. A painting of a single boat on a lake hung on the left-hand wall, and Becca couldn't help thinking that she was that boat. All alone, just her, drifting along, no direction about her at all.

And then, before she could help herself, tears sprang to her eyes and she tried her best to tuck them away, but there was no holding back this meltdown.

"Becca, honey, what happened?"

"You know Nick Hamilton, right?"

Priscilla smiled, clearly well versed in the latest gossip about Nick and Becca. "I do. Though if what I hear is true, not as well as you."

"Well, he's a Hamilton."

"Right . . . the last name sort of clued me in."

"Well, I'm not. And I'm not a Carlisle or a Littleton or anybody important. I'm a Stark."

Priscilla released a slow breath and leaned over her desk so she could see Becca properly. "That's right, you're a Stark. And you should be damn proud of it. What's so wrong with being a Stark?"

"Ever heard that story of the guy shutting down all the power in town on Christmas Eve? Stark. The woman who stole all the toys from the toy drive in the Square because she thought it was a free-for-all? Stark. Every horrible story you've probably heard in this town all concerned someone in my family. We're the joke of the town and the Hamiltons are revered like gods."

"No one decides your worth but you."

Becca slumped back in her chair. "But see, that's not true. The town's already decided that Nick would have to be insane to choose me, and if he does, I should hold on for dear life or else I might lose the best thing to ever happen to me. And maybe he is, but not because he's a Hamilton. That never mattered to me."

"Did it ever occur to you that it never mattered to him that you're a Stark?"

Becca chewed on her lip, considering. "Maybe."

"I'd say definitely. I've lived in this town for twenty years, and that boy has always adored you. Always. Your family name no more matters to him than the color of the sky."

"Still, I'd feel better if I felt like my life had some direction. Like I'm stepping outside the family shadow instead of living in it."

"I see. So that's why you're here. You want a job."

"I've got a job. I want a career."

Priscilla went to work awakening her laptop and humming away as she went through the job list. She peered over. "Any special skills I'm not aware of? Any degrees? Education at all?"

At the mention of education, Becca's chin dipped down a few inches, embarrassment coursing through her. "No. I started my undergraduate degree in nursing but gave it up when Granny became sick."

"And money's not the issue?"

Becca shook her head. "No, I'm good there. This isn't about the money."

"Then why don't you go back to school?"

"I'm thirty-three years old."

"So? People do it all the time." Priscilla typed in something in her laptop and then turned the computer around. "Maybe online classes to begin with? Or if you really want to do nursing, I hear the University of Kentucky has a great program, and it's just in Lexington. You could drive to classes and still work at the diner."

The idea swirled around in Becca's mind, her thoughts trying to make sense of going back to school, being on a college campus with twentysomethings and her so much older. Could she really do it? Could her ego handle it?

"College . . ."

Priscilla grinned at her. "I'll pull together some options for you. Swing back by after your shift. I'll have them all ready."

"But can I really go back to school and start all over?"

Closing her laptop and peering at Becca, Priscilla's expression turned serious. "You'll never get to the end if you refuse to start. Some things are worth putting yourself out there for. You have to decide if this is one of them."

Suddenly, Becca found herself smiling, hope bubbling up. "Could I really do this?"

"You can do anything you want, honey. You just have to make up your mind to try. Are you ready to try?"

"You know . . . I think I am."

Nick walked into his office, every nerve and muscle in his body urging him to turn around and rush over to Becca's. He wanted to lose himself in her lips again, but he needed to figure things out at the office first. Plus, a small part of him was nervous that she'd changed her mind.

The last time he saw her, she was tucking him in at his house after the putt-putt episode, him too drunk to be of any use to anybody. Then he had to hit a plane the next morning for a meeting out in California. They'd spoken on the phone, but it wasn't the same, and he wanted to see her so he could read her expression, see if she was still okay with this.

Whatever this was.

He ran a hand over his face and pushed on, eager to meet with Hamilton Industries controller, Greg, before he did anything else. His meeting with their offices in California had given him hope that maybe they could still salvage the business. California had spoken of some fantastic prospects and ideas that could really turn the business around. But like anything else, those new ideas would take money, and until he spoke with Greg, he had no idea whether those prospects and ideas could be turned into realities. Still, he had hope for the first time in a year and that hope, coupled with the excitement coursing through him at seeing Becca later, made him feel like a renewed man.

Like maybe happiness wasn't a once-in-a-lifetime thing. Maybe he could find it again and again, which sounded ideological and overly philosophical, but he couldn't help it.

"Hey, got a minute?" he asked from outside Greg's office door. The controller had been with the company for as long as Nick could remember, and for as long as he could remember Greg had been gray-haired and hunchbacked.

Greg was on the phone, but he waved him in and motioned to one of the chairs in front of his desk.

"Right, no Stables numbers are solid. Yeah. Nope, good work. It's solid."

Nick tried to ignore the pang in his stomach that Trip had kept Hamilton Stables thriving after their father's death and Nick couldn't do the same with Industries. He replayed some of his riskier decisions over the years, but there was no way of knowing what had caused business to decline. It could be any one of a million things, none of which Nick could predict. And that was one of the main differences between Stables and Industries. Stables had to perform in order to maintain business, but those successes were black and white. They won a title, bred a champion, or they didn't.

Industries wasn't so cut and dried, but that didn't keep Nick from carrying the burden of the state of the business.

"Sorry about that." Greg pushed his phone away from him and threaded his fingers together on the desk. "What can I do for you?"

"That was Trip?"

"Alex, actually."

"Ah." The knot in Nick's stomach tightened still further. Even Alex was turning a profit for the company. What had Nick done so wrong? Why couldn't he turn things around?

He thought of his visit with California again and that tiny morsel of hope bloomed. "So, I just returned from Cali and—"

"It's not going to happen, Nick." Greg's grim expression registered in Nick's mind and he wondered why he hadn't noticed it before.

"But they said—"

"I know what they said. They're wrong. Foolish and wrong."

"Their ideas were—"

"I know."

Nick jumped up, then. "Stop doing that. Stop interrupting me.

Stop treating me like the idiotic kid who never had a chance of making the team. We have prospects here. We can't let the company go without exploring them."

Eyeing the door and the staff outside, all watching them now, Greg closed the door, and then sat back down as calmly as ever, but his intent was clear. "Do you want to bankrupt this company? Is that what you want? Because it would cost millions in research and development to explore those ideas. To realize those prospects. Is that what you want? Because these people are counting on you. You, not me. You. Are you really willing to risk their livelihoods to save your ego?"

"I'm doing this for them."

"No, you're not. Compton agreed to maintain the current staff. And you can have that outlined in the contract. Which you know. This isn't about them. It's about you deluding yourself into believing you've failed your father. The business was declining well before he died. You know that, too."

Nick sighed heavily and took his seat again, this time with the weight of defeat on his shoulders. "What do I do? Let it go? Not try to do everything I can? What kind of man would I be if I let it go without a fight?"

"A smart man. You aren't letting it go. You're selling it. It's business, and this happens every day. Your decision to sell isn't submitting to failure, it's preventing failure. Why can't you see that?"

"I need more time."

"There's no more time. The deal has to close or they'll find another company to buy. You know how these things work."

Nick stood then and started for the door.

"What are you going to do?"

Nick hesitated, his hand on the doorknob, visions of playing in these offices when he was a kid running through his head and hurting his heart. "I . . ." He shook his head. "I need more time."

"Well, hurry. You're right—we are counting on you here. Counting on you to make the right decision."

Nick peered at the controller, who'd been with his father from the beginning, who he'd known all his life. "I know. Trust me, I know."

Chapter Ten

Becca scattered all the college applications Priscilla had pulled for her onto her bed. She had community colleges, liberal art colleges, giant universities, private schools Becca couldn't afford unless she won the lottery. And seeing as how she didn't even play the lottery, that was a long shot.

For as long as she could remember, she'd always wanted to be a nurse. Her mother used to say that doctors flew in and looked like the heroes, but it was the nurses who really deserved the cape. She wasn't entirely sure if that were true until she caught a bad bought of viral pneumonia when she was ten. She was in the hospital for what felt like forever, and her sister was still at home, so while her parents and grandparents were there all the time, it was mostly Granny and the nurses who kept her company.

That was the day she decided she wanted to be a nurse. She wanted to be the superhero without the cape, because the truth was Becca had never cared much about attention or recognition. The cape would never matter to her. She simply wanted to help people, and nursing would allow her to do just that while also getting to know the patients on a more personal level.

She'd worked herself to the bone all through high school to maintain perfect grades, and it had paid off. She was in the top of her class, narrowly missing valedictorian, and had a full ride to Duke, the school of her dreams.

Everything was lined up, her future laid out before her, bright. She'd managed a semester and a half before she got the call that Granny could no longer take care of herself. Immediately, she thought back to those weeks at the hospital when she was ten, Granny refusing to leave her side, and knew what she had to do.

Packing up her dorm and saying good-bye to Duke had been one of the hardest days of her life. And while it had devastated her to leave, she learned through that experience that dreams weren't always a reality for adults. And though she felt the loss of what might have been, she was glad she'd had those years with her grandmother. Her conscience was clear, even if her heart ached for something more than the life she now led.

Now, at thirty-three and not growing a day younger, she felt silly trying to go back to school, starting all over again. Pretending she could just reinvent her life. People were set by the time they reached their thirties, habits ingrained and skill sets mastered—or in Becca's case, not; how could she erase all of that and start again? And even if she was accepted to a school, how would she juggle going to school and working full-time?

It was all too much.

She glanced at the mirror over her dresser, at her reflection, at the photo of her and Nick in high school framed on the dresser. Of the photo of her and her grandmother beside it. They were the only two people in the world who really understood her, and now she and Nick were starting . . . well, whatever they were starting. Things in her life were changing. If ever there was a time to put herself out there, it was now.

A thrill worked through her, and she sorted the college applications into two piles—the schools she for sure wanted to explore and those that were either too expensive or too far away.

With newfound determination, she forced herself to throw caution to the wind and pulled out her laptop. Which immediately made her wish she'd lived in that moment of high for a beat long.

Apparently, her credits from Duke may or may not transfer, depending on the program, and then she would have to apply to schools almost like she was starting from scratch. This was going to be harder than she'd originally thought, and she was already insanely afraid. The application process was one of those things you were forced to do if you wanted to pursue college, but at least once you were accepted to your school of choice it was over.

Now Becca would have to do it all over again. The likelihood of everything coming together seemed slim to none.

Dropping her head onto one of her pillows, she ordered herself to calm down. Anything worth having required work, or however that saying went. This was just part of the work.

Deep breath, she told herself. One thing at a time.

Now on to trying other things.

She eyed the dive gear in the corner of her room. They'd made it through all the classwork and the final pool session was that weekend. So far Becca had managed to float at the surface, unable to release the breath she needed to drop. Zac had assured her they would adjust her weight belt for this weekend, but she was nervous that maybe this was just another thing on the Becca-Is-So-Not-Athletic list. But she was close, so, so close. After this session, all they had left was the checkout dive in open waters, and then she would be officially certified. Scuba diver Becca.

Now that was a title she could get behind.

But if she was being perfectly honest, the checkout dive scared the crap out of her. So she set all her dive stuff in the corner, but in the open, so she'd have to look at it every day. Eventually she felt her brain would just shrug and no longer be deathly afraid. That shrug had yet to happen.

The problem was that she struggled in the pool with the freedom of the surface within reach. How would she handle being feet upon feet below the surface, sharks and other crazy things swimming all around her? In the pool, she was surrounded by other students and Zac, who was trained to make sure they didn't die. And then there was Nick, who she trusted more than anyone else in the world. A part of her wanted to ask Nick to go with her on the dive, but he was already certified and had so much going on at the office. She knew he didn't have the time.

Still . . .

Walking over to the gear, she pulled on the mask and snorkel and stared at her reflection. "What were you thinking, getting into this mess? Clearly not thinking at all."

"Talking to yourself again?"

Becca jumped and spun around, yanking the mask off in one fluid motion, only to see Nick in her doorway instead of the serial killer she'd at first feared.

"Not a serial killer."

Becca scowled. "I didn't say anything."

"You were thinking it."

"I . . . Fine, I was thinking it."

"You don't even lock your front door. And anyway, when was the last murder in Triple Run?" Nick asked. "Oh, right, there's never been one."

Becca walked over and placed the mask and snorkel back with the rest of her gear. "Yeah, well, you know they'd start with me."

Nick laughed and she peered over, the sound sending a shot directly to her heart. Their eyes locked. She had no idea how to act around him. Sure they'd kissed—several times. But kissing did not a boyfriend make. And did he even want to kiss her again? Or be her boyfriend, for that matter?

As if on cue, his gaze dropped to her lips, and she smiled a little.

"I missed you," he said.

"I missed you, too."

They continued to stare at each other, both unsure of what to do next, when Nick motioned to the dive gear. "What's all that?"

"Dive gear."

He rolled his eyes. "I'm tired, not stupid. What's it all doing out?"

Becca fumbled with the snorkel, dropping it on the floor. Yep, she was going to be a pro at diving. At this point, she'd be lucky if she didn't get herself drowned.

"Well, you know how we have just the one pool session next and then the checkout dive to complete our certification?"

"Yeah . . ."

"See, I have to go on the checkout dive."

"So . . ."

"You're going to make me say it, aren't you?"

Nick's mouth quirked up. "You're scared."

"Oh my God, scared is like the understatement of the year here. I'm freaking out-of-my-mind petrified. What if a shark comes up and eats me? What if one of those giant groupers eats me? What if my air dies or whatever and I can't breathe? What if I rush to the surface in a panic and my lungs explode?"

Now he was full-out grinning. "Calm down. It's simple."

"Says the guy who's been on hundreds of dives."

"And I'll be going on one more."

She glanced over at him. "Really?"

"Of course. There's no way I'd let you go alone with an amateur like Zac." At her pointed stare, he relented. "Fine, he's pretty good. But it's still a little scary your first time. Why don't you come over and have dinner with me tonight? At my house. I'll cook and we'll practice in my pool."

"Seriously? That would be amazing. I was hoping to go on the checkout dive with the group next weekend, but I'm freaking myself out."

"Don't bring all that gear, just a swimsuit and the mask and snorkel."

"Swimsuit?" Becca thought of the only bathing suit she had, aside from the damp, chlorine-scented one-piece she wore to dive class—a tiny black bikini that showed way too much skin, and that was years ago, when she didn't have all these extra curves.

Heat filled Nick's eyes as though he realized the same thing as she had—them together, alone, next to no clothes on, in his heated pool. This could get dangerous and fast.

"New fear?"

"You have no idea."

Twenty minutes later, Nick and Becca were in Triple Run Market and More to grab some food for their dinner, Nick's thoughts still on Becca in a swimsuit and whether he'd be able to contain himself once he saw her.

It wasn't the first time he and Becca had been swimming together, but the last time was when they were teens, and though he'd had issues resisting her then, it wasn't the same now. Adult Becca was curvy in all the right places, and his brain was having a hard time concentrating and—

"Nick?"

His head snapped up and he realized he'd been studying those curvy goods right in the middle of the produce section.

Becca grabbed a carrot, and suddenly, Nick was picturing a very different long, hard thing between her hands, and good God, he needed a cold, cold shower.

"Are you all right?" Becca reached out to touch his forehead and he grabbed her hand, threading his fingers through hers, and tugged her toward him. His head tilted toward hers, a smile on his face.

"You are tempting me into oblivion and you're not even doing anything. What the hell am I going to do with myself?"

"Nick, is that you?"

Nick closed his eyes and took a step back from Becca. So close yet so far away. He turned to face Mayor Phillips. "Yes, Mayor. What can I do for you?"

"The trustees and I were just curious whether you planned to attend the festival next weekend?"

"Yes, sir."

"And your brothers?"

"Likely, yes."

"Great." The mayor rocked back on his heels, his gaze traveling between Nick and Becca. "The Square would be a fine choice, just saying."

Nick shook his head. "Just saying what?"

The mayor eyed Becca, and something on her face must have given him pause because he cleared his throat and waved it off. "Nothing. See you Saturday."

"What was that about?" Nick asked as the mayor skirted off, and then his gaze searched around the small grocery story to find every set of eyes on them. "Good God, this is ridiculous."

"You have no idea."

Nick focused on Becca. "What did they do?"

"More what they said. Just that I was lucky to find you and I should get you in a nice suit in front of God and all of Triple Run at the Square."

"Ah, that was the Square comment."

"Yeah. They want a spring wedding."

Nick scoffed. "Wedding? Are they insane?"

"Yeah, clearly. Insane." But Becca's voice didn't quite match her words, and Nick peered over, a hint of fear dripping into his happy mood. Did Becca want this to go that far? Surely not; they were just starting whatever they were starting. They hadn't even talked about what this was, where it was going, or any one of a thousand other conversations they should have.

"We're good, right?" he asked, stopping her before she went on to the meats.

A smile took over her face. "We're great."

Then, before anyone else bothered him, he leaned in to press a quick kiss to her lips, and instantly, he wanted to do it again, take it further, see if he could drive her as crazy as she was driving him. He tucked her hair behind her ear and trailed his fingers through the long strands. "I like this."

"Me too." She smiled again, and then, town be damned, he took her hand and they continued their shopping that way, sure the whole town was getting a show, but for once, Nick couldn't care less.

They decided on steaks, baked potatoes, grilled zucchini, and salad, because Becca could out eat a linebacker. It was one of the things he loved most about her, and though he caught the apprehension on her face at the idea of being in a swimsuit in front of him, he knew at heart she was okay with who she was. Becca was Becca, and he never wanted her to change.

"Swim first?" Nick asked as he parked in his garage.

"Sure." Becca stepped out and went around to help with the groceries, but Nick waved her off.

"No, ma'am. You go get changed and ready yourself to become the best scuba diver on the planet. I'll handle this."

"Are you sure?"

"Absolutely."

With obvious reluctance, Becca grabbed her tote and disappeared inside his house. He knew it took effort for her to let go, to allow someone else to take care of her, but she deserved it. Becca had spent her whole life taking care of others—her grandmother, her sister, her niece and nephew. It was time someone took care of her, and though Nick had tried to help where he could over the years, they were different now—more—and he was going to take care of her whether she liked it or not.

Setting down the bags in the kitchen, he went to work putting everything away, until his gaze caught Becca walking around the pool, already changed, the mask and snorkel dangling in her hand, and the tiniest excuse for a bikini he'd ever seen on her body. And suddenly Nick was very, very thankful for whoever designed that bikini, because holy hell.

Without her awareness to keep him in check, he took her in. Her full breasts, spilling out of the swimsuit top, the dip and curve of her waist, her flat, toned stomach, her wide hips and long, long legs. Suddenly, Nick regretted ever making fun of her for buying that infomercial twenty-five-minute workout set, because while he knew Becca was beautiful, he never knew what she hid under those T-shirts and tank tops she wore.

With the quickness of a man in need, he shoved the rest of the groceries into the fridge and jogged back to his room, eager to change and get out there, though hell if he'd know what to do once he got there.

He planned to take this slow, to get to know her in this new way, but already he wanted to take her to his bed, forget all the complications and show her over and over again the way she deserved to be treated. Worship her body until she forgot every man before him.

But that was his stupid side talking—all right, his horny side. Slow was better, even if it killed him.

He splashed several rounds of cold water on his face, tugged off his clothes, and put on his swim trunks, giving himself a pep talk throughout the change that he would be good—slow and good.

Damn, even that sounded sexy as hell to his ears now.

He was going to die before this night was over.

Grabbing two bottles of water and a couple of beers, he opened the French doors off his kitchen and padded out onto the patio and to the pool. Becca hadn't noticed him yet, so he snuck up and pressed one of the bottles of water to her exposed neck. Immediately, she squealed and spun around, causing her breasts to jump in that tiny top, Nick's gaze to drop, and his restraint to flounder.

"Easily startled, as always."

Becca opened her mouth to pop off at him, but her eyes went to his chest and down his abs, and he grinned a little at the realization that she was as affected by him as he was her. He said a silent thank you that he'd spent the last few years in the gym every day, working off all the thoughts and emotions he couldn't speak. It was a lonely endeavor, but he was in good shape because of it.

"Should we get started?" she asked, swallowing hard and eyeing him.

"Depends what you want to get started." Nick took a step toward her, his eyes dropping to her bikini. "I gotta say, at this point, with you in that, I'd do pretty much anything you wanted."

Her cheeks reddened and she drew a breath. "I know, it's too small, but I didn't know that when I brought it. Seems I haven't worn a bikini in a while." She adjusted the top and her breasts bobbed again.

Nick swallowed hard. "Let's get in the water before I get myself in trouble."

They walked over to the steps, each careful not to touch the other, the whole thing ridiculous, but at this point they were in survival mode.

The water was warm thanks to the heater, but it was doing little to cool off his raging hormones.

"Okay, so put on the mask and make sure it's tight," he said, refusing to look at her. He needed a minute to settle down or all ideas of slow were going to fly away—along with their swimsuits.

"Is this good?"

He turned around to face her, the giant mask covering her face, a smile bigger than all of Triple Run just below it, and that was it. "I have to kiss you. Just once." He moved in before she could say anything, quickly kissed her lips, and groaned as he pulled away. "All right, twice."

Their lips met for a second time, and with a slow, long moan of her own, telling him that she wasn't eager to remain on the good side if he couldn't hold back. Just as he started to deepen the kiss, she jerked the mask off and tossed it in the water. And then there was nothing between them, nothing to keep this from going too far.

"Bec . . ."

"Kiss me."

His hands wrapped around her again, securing her to him, as his mouth found hers and his tongue slid over her lips, then inside her mouth, flicking over the mint on her tongue, and then his hands were on her back, reaching down to grab her ass and pull her to him.

All control flew up into the night sky, the stars their only cover, and he moved from her lips to her neck to her collarbone, tasting and licking, each sound driving him insane.

She tilted her head back, her breasts pushing up, and then his head dipped down, his tongue gliding over the swell of her breasts, her sounds destroying him more and more with each touch. He pushed aside one triangle and her full breast popped out, her soft pink nipple calling to him, and suddenly he was there—gone. All restraint absolutely gone.

He pressed his mouth to her nipple, sucking it into his mouth, and the moan she released was enough to make him want her right there, sure he wouldn't make it out of the pool without claiming her as his. He wrapped her legs around his waist and moved to the edge of the pool, her body pressed against the wall, as he took his time sucking and tasting, his hand freeing her other breast so they were both exposed, ready for him to pleasure and enjoy. Good God, she was beautiful.

And all his.

The thought warmed him in ways the rest never could. This beautiful, amazing woman was his. And he had no intention of letting her go. Fear be damned, and now it was time he gave her what she needed.

He glided a hand over her hip, inside her thigh, and then he pushed aside her bikini bottoms and stroked her heat. She bucked against him, eager and ready, and he slipped a finger inside her, then a second, driving her closer and closer to her release.

"Nick, God. I . . ." His kissed her hard, pushing every bit of the emotion he felt into that moment until finally he felt her body quivering as she reached her climax. He brought her back down slowly and she fell slack against him, her breathing heavy. "That was . . . I don't even know what to say."

He kissed her temple. "That was just the beginning." She reached down to his swim trunks and he took her hand, stopping her. "Not today. This was just about you."

"Nick . . ."

"I know what you're going to say, but no one takes care of you. Let me take care of you." He kissed her lips sweetly. "But I think our lesson might be over for today," he said with a grin. "There's some warm towels in the bin beside the fire pit. Go get changed and I'll make dinner."

Becca started away, then turned back, a wide grin on her face. "If that was our first lesson, what do you have in store for lesson two?"

"Prepare yourself, Becca Stark; you're about to meet a new Nick Hamilton." He winked at her, and she laughed before disappearing into the house, leaving Nick in the pool to settle down, happy for the first time in a long, long time.

Chapter Eleven

"All right, today let's talk about how easy it is to go on a check-out dive."

It was Saturday already, and Zac stood outside the pool, the class all inside, half of them, including Becca, shaking like crazy. The temperature of the pool was much colder than it had been during their last session. Or maybe they were just that terrified.

"To illustrate this point, I have a few assistants here to help me today. Come on out, guys."

The set of heavy double doors opened loudly, the sound echoing through the gym. All attention went to the left, and Becca grinned as Charlie and Brady came out, their arms draped around a little girl. The girl was all long blond hair and freckles and adorable smile, and Becca wondered how they knew her, when the guys reached Zac and he bent down to give the girl a hug that lasted a beat too long.

"Dad," the girl whined. "I'm an instructor today."

The Littletons all laughed, but Becca's mind stopped at *dad*. Did she say Dad?

Becca compared the two, her gaze flicking back and forth, scrutinizing. The similarities weren't overly obvious, but they were there— her eyes, perhaps. Or maybe it was the smile that never left her face, so much like her father's. So when Zac said, "Everyone, I'd like you to meet my daughter, Carrie-Anne," Becca wasn't shocked as much as curious.

She'd seen the guys around the diner several times, but never once had Carrie-Anne been with them. Now, in Zac's defense, they usually stopped by during school hours, so maybe that was part of it. But Becca felt there was more to the story.

"Carrie-Anne, can you tell the class how old you are?"

"Thirteen," she said, grinning. She wore a pink wet suit and a pink mask rested on the top of her head, the snorkel dangling.

"And how long have you been certified to dive?"

"Since I was eight."

A hush fell over the class as they all stared at the little girl like she was one of those insanely talented kids who became doctors at five or whatever.

"It's scary at first, but the more you go, the better it gets. And it's so cool. You'll see so many things."

Zac patted her head affectionately, and she shot him an I'm-not-a-baby warning. But instead of him giving her a harder time like some fathers might—like Nick would if he were Carrie-Anne's father—he stepped back and allowed Brady and Charlie to help her into her weight belt, BCD, air tank, and fins. She slid her mask and snorkel into place, and Zac double-checked its fit. "Ready?" Zac asked.

"Ready," she said with a giant smile, and then she jumped into the water, and for a moment, Becca fought the urge to go after her. Surely a girl that small shouldn't stay down for so long, air tank or not. But then she realized she wasn't coming back up. She had air; she had everything she needed.

Charlie and Brady followed suit and Becca found herself relaxing for the first time since Nick had called to tell her he couldn't make it to the session. His voice had been tense as he explained that a random meeting had popped up that he couldn't miss, and she of course said it was fine. But inside, she wanted to scream, *no, come with me, keep me protected.*

But as she took in the thirteen-year-old swimming underwater like a fish, she realized it was stupid to be so afraid of diving. Zac's point was clear—if little Carrie-Anne could do it, anyone could.

With renewed purpose, Becca went through all the techniques Zac had taught her. Then Zac himself approached, and she lost her nerve under his scrutiny.

"Missing your partner?"

"Yeah, he had a meeting this afternoon, and he's already certified, so." She shrugged. Then, desperate to change the subject, she added, "Your daughter seems so sweet. And brave."

Zac glanced at the water, where Carrie-Anne was working with

Brady and Charlie to help some of the others in the class. "Yeah, about that . . . I'm sure you're wondering why I didn't tell you."

"It crossed my mind," Becca said with a grin. "But it's not my business, and in a town full of gossips, I try not to pry."

"It's not prying. Carrie-Anne is the most important thing in the world to me, but her mother left when she was little, and it hurt her badly. So I try to limit interaction between her and women I'm dating, or trying to date. Not so successfully in your case." He laughed, but his voice was tinged with disappointment.

Becca cringed, wishing she'd never hinted at more with Zac. Her heart belonged to Nick, and no one else ever would have worked for her. "Yeah, sorry about that."

"It's my own fault. I called it the moment I met you. You just hadn't realized yet what the rest of us knew from the beginning—Nick worships you."

"Oh, no. He's . . . well, I don't know. We've known each other a long time."

"He's lucky."

Becca glanced over at Carrie-Anne. "So is she. And I think it's wonderful that you try to protect her. That's what I would do if I were in your shoes."

"Really? I'm glad to hear it. It can make dating a challenge, but she's my priority. I want her life to be as stable as possible, ya know?"

"I think it sounds like you're an amazing father. And dive instructor, apparently. She's back under." Becca laughed until she realized Zac wasn't.

"Which brings us to why we're here. It's time you go under now, too. I know you're afraid. I can see it all over your face, but I'm right here. Brady and Charlie are here to help, too. And all of us have been through CPR certification. We won't let anything happen to you."

Becca chewed on her bottom lip. "What if there are sharks?"

A smile pulled at Zac's lips, and Becca thought he was so adorable. She hoped he would find a match for him and Carrie-Anne soon. He deserved happiness. "I know Brady's a little aggressive, but a shark? That's giving him a little too much credit."

Now Becca was laughing hard, relaxing more with each second. Until she thought of the sharks again. "You know what I mean. What if we run into sharks during the checkout dive? I think I'm afraid to complete this last session because it means I have to go out in open water to finish my certification. And I'm scared. Like insanely, might-melt-down scared. Are you sure you want that kind of liability on your hands?"

"Okay, truth time. Have I swum with sharks? Sure. But you have to remember, you're bigger than most of the sharks you'll see, and the rule in the ocean is that nothing bothers anything bigger than it. But even the big sharks want nothing to do with you. They may swim by, but they'll ignore you and keep on trucking. The only time I've run into anything with sharks was when I was spearfishing and a shark snagged a fish from my net. But otherwise? Nothing."

"And piranhas?"

"Have teeth, yes. But again, nothing for you to worry about."

"And if my air dies out?"

"That doesn't happen."

"All right, a hose bursts?"

"That's why you always dive with a buddy, but even then, that's rare, and we'll all be down there with you."

Becca glanced over the pool; everyone in the class was practicing underwater. Everyone except her. Was she really going to be shown up by the elderly man in the class? By little Carrie-Anne?

No.

"I'll go down with you. I'll be right there. And then Nick will be there on the checkout dive, right?"

Becca nodded.

"Okay, then. You're safe. I promise you that you're safe."

With one more swift nod, Becca slipped on her mask, which she'd pushed onto the top of her head, and nodded again to Zac.

"Ready?"

"Yes." *No.*

Zac released the air in his BCD and began to sink. Becca did the same, her heart hammering like crazy in her chest, but she ignored it. This wasn't going to beat her. Not this. Not going back to college.

She could do anything she wanted to do, age be damned, fear be damned.

Finally, she sank below the surface, and Zac gave her an okay gesture and she offered it back, and then she was swimming. Underwater. Breathing. Underwater. The whole thing felt so surreal that before she thought better of it, she sped up, her breathing labored, and she realized she was using too much of her air supply. Slowing down, she took her time exploring the props Zac had placed in the bottom of the pool, checking her air constantly along the way. And then, too quickly, Zac swam over and gave her the thumbs-up that it was time to go back up.

She broke the surface and squealed, excitement coursing through her, mixing with pride.

"You did great," Zac said. "See, you're ready for the checkout dive. It's the same thing."

Brady draped an arm around her shoulder. "Yep, the same. Just watch out for the sharks."

Nick toyed with his cell phone, rotating it around and around, part of him wishing he'd never asked for the appointment, the other half eager for it to begin.

He told himself that he was doing due diligence, double-checking all the things he needed to double-check, crossing his Ts and dotting his Is. But really, he wanted to see if he still felt the same comfort he'd felt the last time he'd met the man.

The elevator pinged loudly on the quiet floor, and Nick set his phone down on his desk and glanced out his open doorway, only to find the crew had come by for the weekly cleaning.

With a deep breath, he leaned back in his chair and took in his office. Never had an office looked less like its owner than this one. For whatever reason, he'd never wanted his degree to be hung there, when it had always been a huge deal to his parents. So for years his diplomas had hung in the study of his parents' house. Only when they had both passed had he moved it, and now it was in his office at his house: an office that exuded his personality.

Part of the problem was that Nick had left the decorating of his office at home to Becca and the one at work to the decorator on the project. One person knew him; the other cared only about money.

So his work office was full of expensive drapes and furnishings and other things that meant nothing to Nick.

His home office was comfortable, the desk itself nothing to write home about, but the chair was meant for a man to sit in and work. God, he loved that chair. And if this meeting went the way he both feared and hoped, that might be his permanent office going forward.

Well, at least he had the chair.

The elevator pinged again, and Nick glanced up in time to watch William Compton step off. He swallowed hard, but he didn't stand to greet the man. He wanted to prove a point—this was his decision, and though he'd immediately liked Compton, even if he hated to admit it, he didn't know the man and therefore refused to trust him.

So Nick watched him walk toward his office, but where most men might arrogantly ask what this was all about, William stopped in the doorway and knocked, despite the door being open.

"Mr. Hamilton? You asked to see me."

"Call me Nick, and I did. Please, come in." When Compton stared down the hall to the conference room, Nick added, "That was my father's conference room. If it's okay, I'd rather not discuss selling his business in the place where he helped it thrive."

Compton nodded slowly and took one of the chairs in front of Nick's desk, watching him in a way that made him uneasy, yet the look was so familiar that he couldn't help getting straight to the point.

"Mr. Compton, I—"

"Surely if you insist that I call you Nick, you can call me William."

Once again, Nick thought that he liked William Compton, that something about him felt real in a world of fake. "William. I'll be honest with you. I didn't call you here so much to talk about selling you the business as asking why you want it."

"I should think that would be obvious."

"With most of the investors who've sought us out, yes. But not you. I get the impression there's a reason you're here, and it has nothing to do with business. What's the story?"

William stood then and started around the office, stopping at a large portrait on the wall of Carter with his three sons. "He was very proud of you, Nick. Talked about you all the time. 'Nick's going to conquer the world,' he used to say."

"I thought you might know my father, but that isn't what has me confused. You can't be in this business without knowing Carter Hamilton. But what I can't figure out is why you also look like him. It's barely there, and you could argue that all older men look the same. Hell, you could argue that all young men look the same. But there's something about you in particular that I can't quite put my finger on."

William sat back in his chair, his elbow propped up on the armrest as he studied Nick, and then a smile broke across his face. "He always said you were the smartest."

"So you did know him."

At that, William laughed. "Yes, I'd say I did. He was my brother, after all."

"Your what?" Nick's mouth fell open, and though he prided himself on his composure in meetings, he couldn't force it back closed.

"I see that's come as a bit of a shock to you, which isn't surprising. Carter was a private man, as you know. And he would never have wanted to taint the memory you have of your grandfather. I daresay I didn't know him as well and am not so loyal."

"I don't understand."

"Carter was my half brother. Your grandfather was my father. He had an affair with my mother who, as cliché as it might be, was his assistant. They maintained a relationship for many years before my mother married the man I considered to be my father all my life."

"But why didn't you tell me that during that first meeting?"

William offered a warm smile. "It wasn't my secret to tell."

Nick tried to make sense of what William was saying, but he came up empty. What he knew of Frank Hamilton was that his grandfather had been a strong businessman, forever driven, but also a family man, much more so than even Carter had been. The idea of him having an affair seemed farfetched and offensive.

But then Nick thought of his times visiting Frank at the office as a kid, and how different he acted there. Like he led two separate lives. So either Frank was a cheater with two families—one he claimed, one he didn't—or William Compton was a liar.

Nick wasn't ready to taint his memory of his grandfather on the word of a man he barely knew.

"You have your own company, a successful one. Why would you want to buy Hamilton Industries? Is it an ego thing? Buy the business from the father who refused to claim you as his own?"

William laughed, his belly jiggling, his cheeks reddening. "Perhaps I was rash in my assertion of your intellect. Frank did claim me, and I was given the very same opportunities as Carter. But I was never a Hamilton, and I was proud to be a Compton. Years later, Carter and I became friends, and we made an agreement to buy the other's business before allowing it to crumble. So here I am."

"But my father passed away five years ago. There's no reason for you to honor your agreement."

"That's where you're wrong. The person you are, the impact you make, the choice to be honorable or not, doesn't have an expiration date. Your existence remains for eternity. Your mark on this world will never fade and you have a choice—be remembered for the good or for the bad. Either way, someone *will* remember you. I'd prefer to stay on the good side; wouldn't you?"

The longer Nick spoke to William, the more he felt as if he was talking to his father. He spoke like him, their voices similar, the way they used every conversation to interject some bit of age-old wisdom. And the longer he thought about it, the more his gut told him to trust William. What could he possibly gain from lying? Nothing. "Trip and Alex don't know."

"Nor do my sons. Nor would you, if you hadn't figured it out."

"You could have lied."

"We just went over that."

Nick laughed then, relaxing into his chair. "So this isn't a greedy businessman trying to buy my father's business. It's my . . . uncle? You'll forgive my doubts."

"You wouldn't be a Hamilton if you trusted me at my word alone." William checked his watch and then stood up. "I'm sorry to cut this short, but I have a flight to catch. Doubts are there for a reason—they force us to do our homework. Feel free to do yours, and when you do, I'll be ready to chat again."

Nick stood and shook William's hand. "Thank you for agreeing to meet me. I'll be in touch."

"I hope so." William made it two steps before turning back. "There was an unauthorized biography written about your grandfather, right?"

"There was." Though Nick had never read it.

"When doing your research, you might find it interesting."

Nick nodded to him, and William walked out just as Nick's cell vibrated against his desk. He peered down to find a new text from Becca.

Checkout dive, here I come. I hope you're not planning to back out on me!

Nick thought of his best friend and how much she meant to him, now more than ever. His family might not be the rock he'd always thought it to be, but Becca was as pure as they came, her friendship never wavering.

I wouldn't miss it.

Chapter Twelve

The boat rocked again, throwing Becca forward, and for the first time in her life she understood the term *seasickness*. In all her experiences on a boat, she'd only ever coasted lazily—ocean or lake—but this was something else entirely. And though she wanted to be brave, she had considered asking them to take her back to the marina.

"Are you all right?" Zac asked from her right side, and then Nick on her left added, "Yeah, are you all right?"

The tension between them wasn't quite what it had been before the putt-putt match, but she could still feel that uneasiness between the men. Or maybe the uneasiness she felt was simply part of her sour stomach.

"Fine. Are we almost there?"

"It's just a thirty-minute boat ride from the marina. We're almost there."

Becca nodded, telling—no, ordering—herself to pull it together. She was going on this dive, she would not chicken out, and when she was done, she was going to go back to her and Nick's hotel room and go all dominatrix on him to prove she was the ultimate badass now. So there, fear. Take that!

All right, so maybe there was no way in hell she would ever do the dominatrix thing, but they were going to have sex. Lots of sex. All night. Because it had been a week since that episode in his pool, her putty in his hands, and she was dying to know what he could do in bed if he managed all that amazingness in the pool.

Their schedules hadn't lined up all week, but now they were in the Florida Keys for the checkout dive, sharing a hotel room, and nothing would ruin this weekend.

Nothing except Becca vomiting all over Nick, which was entirely possible if the boat didn't stop soon.

Deep breath.

"Are you sure you're okay?" Nick asked when Zac went to the front of the boat to talk to the captain. With their charter service, they weren't the only class on the boat, and Becca found herself studying each of the other students, in her class and the others, curious as to who was the weakest link. Who wouldn't go through with it. And she'd come to the unfortunate conclusion that none of them appeared as scared as she felt. So if they were ranking the coolest to the uncoolest, she was at the slap bottom. Number one on the uncool list.

If she didn't go through with the dive, she would be that lady. The one twiddling her thumbs, dressed in full dive gear, only to watch others having all the fun. Was she really going to let that happen? After all, she had faced things in her life and never once had she backed down. So fear or not, she would do this. She would jump in that water and suck up every doubt and dive, dammit.

Her stomach lurched again.

If she didn't throw up first.

Finally, the boat stopped in the middle of the ocean, water all around, and Becca remembered that *I'm Alive* show she'd watched during the summer, in which that couple's boat sank and they were on that tiny life raft, surrounded by sharks, and the man's leg was bitten off, and their lips were all crinkly from lack of water and their skin was burned by the sun—

"Becca? You're white."

She shook her head. "No. It's the lighting, the sun. I'm fine."

"Bec . . ."

"I'm doing this."

Nick grinned and leaned into her, kissing her cheek, then whispering in her ear, "You're adorable when you're determined."

She smiled and the nervous rope cutting off her air supply loosened a bit. "You won't leave me?"

"Nope, it's the buddy system. You never leave your buddy. I won't leave you."

She drew a long breath. "Thank you. For coming. For everything."

"Nowhere else I'd rather be. Now let's get your tank set up."

They spent the next few minutes following Zac's instructions. Fasten on weight belt. Place the BCD on the tank, the regulator on top, turn the air on, listen for leaks, turn it back off, but remember to turn it on before jumping in the water.

Becca had just sat back down, feeling better about the whole thing, everything she'd learned and all the hard work over the last six weeks playing out, when Zac stood up. "All right, let's get ready. Strap into your tanks."

Okay, you can do this. You can do this. Don't look at the water yet, don't think about sharks. Oh, shit, I thought about sharks. Sharks, sharks, sharks. Oh my God, I'm going to be in the water with sharks.

"Becca, try to relax."

"I'm relaxed," she said without looking at Nick." Totally chill. I've got this."

If the sharks don't get me.

She sat down and slipped into her BCD, then slid on her fins, and suddenly it was her turn.

It was her turn.

Drawing up every bit of her courage, she smiled at Nick as he went before her, and then she went to stand, and immediately snapped back onto the bench. "Woah!" She tried to stand again and snapped back yet again. Oh my God. She was too weak to carry all the gear, she was a failure even before she got into the water. But then, she'd carried all the gear during their pool lessons, so it couldn't be that. Still, she tried to stand again, only to remain fixed on the bench.

"Nick, help," she called after trying for the fourth time. He turned around and burst out laughing.

"What?"

"You dressed your tank with the bungee cord on instead of unstrapping it first, then restrapping it."

"English, please?"

He opened his mouth, but she must have shot him a shut-the-hell-up-and-help-me look because he quickly closed his mouth. "No big deal. Rookie mistake." He waddled over to her while the rest of the class tapped their feet and sighed in annoyance. Nick removed the regulator block from the top of the tank, unstrapped the bungee cord from the tank, and then put it all back together again.

Ah, now Becca understood the whole unstrapping and restrapping comments. She was such an idiot.

"There you go, madame," he said, the widest smile in the world on his face. "All set now."

"Shut up."

"I didn't say anything."

She stood up, and the weight of the equipment, the balance change, and the rocking boat nearly had her falling back over, but Nick caught her. It took every ounce of her patience to say "Thank you" when he was so obviously fighting to keep from laughing.

"All right, we're up." Becca followed after Nick, watched him take the wide step Zac had taught them in the pool off the boat and into the water.

He popped up from the water and spun around to give the captain the diver gesture for okay, and then all eyes were on Becca.

She waddled to the back of the boat and then, before she could chicken out, she took the wide step off the boat and dropped into the water.

Cold water hit her hands and face, but her wet suit worked to keep the majority of her body comfortable. She spun in the water and gave the captain the go gesture.

"Game time," Nick said, smiling at her.

"I'm ready," she said, her teeth chattering a bit from nervousness and excitement. Because she was excited. The whole thing had a thrill factor to it, and she was eager to see the experience through.

Nick instructed her to release the air from her BCD and then, slowly, she began to sink into the water. At first, fear worked through her again, all the visions flashing before her eyes. But then she told herself to breathe, she could breathe, the regulator was working, she was okay.

She dropped lower and lower, careful to remember to swallow every few feet to clear her ears, until she reached the group. And that was when she first noticed the coral, a thousand colors, each one more unique than the last. The fish. Schools and schools of fish. And then the last of her worry dripped away and she was left with nothing but awe.

They explored the coral, careful not to touch or damage it. They swam around and through fish of every imaginable color and shape and size. And no sharks in sight. Not even one!

Too soon, Nick gave her the thumbs-up that it was time to go back up. Thirty minutes had passed in the blink of an eye.

Becca followed Nick's lead to go up slowly to protect her lungs, and then she broke free on the surface, a laugh bubbling up from the thrill of it all. She wanted to go back down, explore for hours and hours, but she knew the dive time was up. The current was rough so as she approached the ladder, Nick helped her hand over her fins and then Zac and another woman from her class helped her up the ladder and into the boat.

Finally, Nick was in the boat, too, and she wrapped her arms around him, kissing him hard, right there before the class and the clouds and God. She didn't care. For once, she didn't care about anything or anyone else—just the man, her friend, who had turned her life upside down the moment he said he wanted her.

"That was unbelievable."

He grinned and kissed her again. "We'll make an athlete of you yet."

Becca pulled back. "Now let's not get crazy here. An athlete Becca Stark is not, but I love this. Can we go again tomorrow?"

"We'll go as often as you like. Just wait until you dive in Fiji."

"Wow, Fiji."

"Maybe we could go in the spring."

A smile played on her lips, but she couldn't help it. "Are you making future plans with me, Nick Hamilton?"

He smiled back. "Yeah . . . I guess I am."

Nick took his time in the shower, his thoughts confusing and yet clear. He thought of Becca's question again—*are you planning a future with me?*—and all he could think was yes, he absolutely wanted a future with her.

So why did the idea of it scare the hell out of him?

He told himself he didn't have to worry about it for now; they were together and his heart was happy, and for now that was all that mattered. Them, together. Because the idea of losing Becca now could break him for good. Their friendship was important to him, but he knew in his heart that there was no one else for him. Becca was his match.

He wrapped a towel around his waist and padded out of the bathroom, only to find Becca in her bra and panties, not yet dressed from her own shower. There was nothing overly sexy about the getup—

turquoise bra and turquoise panties, both with white lace trim—yet suddenly Nick couldn't think about anything but the last time his hands had been on her. His mouth on her.

As though she could feel his stare, her gaze switched from the clothes laid out on the bed to him.

"Um, hey, I didn't expect you to come out so soon. I didn't know what we were doing for dinner, so I set out two outfits—dressy-ish or casual—but I gotta tell you, I'm exhausted and . . ." Her eyes drifted down his chest like she was seeing him clearly for the first time. Her gaze trailed over his stomach to the white towel wrapped around his waist.

In two easy steps he reached her. "Or we could stay in."

"Or we could stay in," she repeated.

All Nick could think was that he should be nervous, he should be hesitant, he should have fear or worry or some emotion that told him to pause the moment and think. But as his eyes fell back on Becca's, all he could think was that this was where he should be, where he belonged. He didn't have the strength to fight it anymore.

Closing the distance between them, Nick tilted her chin up and stared into those endlessly kind eyes of hers. "You were amazing today."

"I loved it."

"Absolutely amazing." He pressed a kiss to her lips, then her neck, then trailed them over her shoulder, dropping her bra strap in the process. "And absolutely beautiful." He continued the kiss across her chest, slipping off the other strap, then the bra was unfastened and falling to the floor.

"We can wait," he said, eager to make sure she was comfortable. That she knew this was more to him than a fling. It was everything.

"No . . . we can't."

Nick pressed his lips to hers and eased her back down on the bed, dropping his towel in the effort.

Becca's gaze found him and she reached for him, stroking him slowly, her touch driving him insane.

"I want you inside me," she breathed. That was all the permission he needed; he slid her panties off, pressing hot kisses along her stomach as he went, then over her hip, down her thigh. He stared down at her mound as he stroked her, a finger slipping inside.

"Nick, now . . . please."

He smiled to himself as he stepped away from her and reached for a condom from his carry-on bag, tore the silver wrapping, and rolled it on. His eyes fell back on her as he drove inside, and then they were together and he kissed her with a new passion, full of new words he couldn't say—words of commitment and their future. Words of love.

Her body tightened and stars crested his vision, his heart out of control as he released inside her, this woman who had been his everything for most of his life. And he couldn't help thinking that he'd had it all wrong before.

This was happiness.

Chapter Thirteen

The day was impossibly bright, the sky cloudless and blue, the birds singing their salute to the morning. And Becca couldn't stop smiling.

She stretched in bed and glanced at the time, only to realize she'd woken an hour earlier than usual. For as long as Becca could remember, her natural wake-up time was eight o'clock. Whether she went to bed at ten P.M. or two A.M., she woke at eight in the morning. But today she was up at seven, and not just awake but energized and ready for her day. Like something huge was about to happen and she couldn't remain in bed another second. And that something went by the name Nick Hamilton.

A tingly sensation spiraled through her belly at the thought of him, and she smiled wide. Butterflies. Becca Stark, waitress extraordinaire, had butterflies.

It was all too much.

So to force herself to stop being silly and go about her day like it was just another normal day, not the first day that she and Nick were together-together in Triple Run—she pushed out of bed and wrapped her favorite fleece robe around her. The morning air held all the chill of fall and Becca's grin widened. She loved fall. She loved mornings. She loved every single thing about this day. But mostly, she loved that she could finally show her true feelings around Nick.

No more glancing away when he changed shirts because she didn't want to get caught checking him out. No more uncomfortable silences when he talked about dates. No more embarrassment at being caught saying his name in her sleep. Granted, that had happened only the one time after she'd fallen asleep on his couch during a movie, but it had taken Nick six months to stop chiding her about it.

She shuffled into her kitchen, flicked on the light, and then quickly pressed the Power button on her ancient Mr. Coffee coffeemaker three times to get it to turn on. Finally, the little green light was lit and Becca sighed with relief. Every morning she came into her kitchen, pressed the coffeemaker Power button three times, and every morning she held her breath until the light came on. Because what in the hell would she do at seven or eight in the morning if it decided it'd had enough of her shenanigans and quit for good? But then, how stupid was it to worry about whether she could make a cup of coffee or not? No one kept around a coffeemaker as old as this one, and no one put up with a coffeemaker that required you to press the Power button three times before it turned on. So why should she?

She shouldn't.

Once the coffee was brewing, she sat down at her kitchen table, pulled out her laptop, and went to Walmart.com. At first, she sorted coffeemakers by price and was prepared to select something less than twenty dollars, but then her gaze locked on a Keurig, and as she read each delicious detail, she found herself going through all the reasons she needed a Keurig in her life. Less waste. Quicker output. Awesome coffee. Super cool features and a thousand different K-Cup flavors.

With a quick search to check prices, she watched as a dozen options populated the screen, each price point more offensive than the last. She moved her mouse to the little X, convinced she couldn't pay that much when hers still worked.

But then she decided *screw that*. She had money in the bank, paid her bills on time, and worked forty to fifty hours per week. She shouldn't have to press the Power button three times on her coffeemaker to get a cup of coffee. That was crap, and she was ready to give herself the things she deserved. Because she did deserve things. Nice things. Her whole life had been for others, and it was time she did something for herself.

Starting with the Keurig.

She found the one she liked, midpriced because though she wanted the thing, she wasn't ready to throw two hundred dollars at it.

"So there." Then she decided that she could use some new towels in her bathroom and added a few of those. And why not a new quilt set for her bed? And oh, oh, new sheets were a must.

Finally, after an hour of searching and adding things, that smile of hers cemented in place, she went to her shopping cart to pay and snapped back.

All right, a thousand dollars spent at Walmart might be excessive.

So she went through and chose the things she really needed, including the Keurig, and some of those fancy K-Cups because she wasn't sure the market carried them. Then, content with her accomplishment so early in the day, she went to her coffeemaker, poured some into her favorite mug, added some sugar and hazelnut creamer, then went back to sit in her chair.

The application for University of Kentucky was still up in browser, taunting her to stop thinking and just do it. Do or die. It was a phrase her daddy used to use all the time, forever the doer—and never the saver—but there was something to it.

Taking a sip of her coffee, she moved the mouse to her favorites and hovered over the University of Kentucky application. She'd taken the SAT and had the scores sent there automatically. They might be there right now, everything in place, ready for her to apply. But could she really do this? Could she go to school with kids ten years younger than her, go back and forth between Triple Run and Lexington, work a forty-plus-hour week while getting her degree?

She pictured herself in nurses' scrubs, caring for a little girl in the hospital as those nurses had cared for her.

Yes. Yes, she could. And it was time to stop thinking about all the things she couldn't do and focus instead on all the things she *could* do.

With one giant breath in and out to push away the fear and another long sip of coffee, she filled out the application, unsure about half of it. Her nerves coiled tight as she read through each question and doubt settled over her. What if she went to all this trouble and didn't get in?

But she *had* gotten into Duke years ago, and her grades there were fantastic. That counted for something, right? She'd had her transcripts transferred, and Kentucky might have those now.

The whole thing was coming together and the last step was to do this, apply. But maybe she wouldn't get in, maybe they would take one look at *waitress* and *thirty-three-year-old* and laugh their asses off.

But she had to try.

Closing her eyes, she hit Send. Done. No going back now.

As if on cue, Becca heard her screen door rap shut and turned in time to find Reagan beside her, narrowly slamming into her face.

"Does that say 'application sent' like a college application?"

Becca closed her laptop and pushed out of her chair to go make another cup of coffee. "So what if it did?"

Reagan crossed her arms, her dark hair pulled back in a ponytail like always, hints of gray peeking out at her temples. "But you're old now. Old people don't go to college."

"They can if they want to." And then she caught the other thing her sister had said and pointed at her. "And I'm not old."

Reagan's eyebrow shot up in mock question, and Becca hated her sister a little bit in that moment for always being able to master sass. "Older than me."

"That doesn't make me old. And maybe you need to worry about yourself going back to college. Or that husband of yours." Becca poured her coffee, mixed in her cream and sugar, then did the same for her sister, her ears pricked for the long sigh she knew would come at the mention of her sister's husband.

A part of Becca felt like the worst sister on the planet for bringing up Reagan's crappy husband, but she needed the attention away from her. In truth, it wouldn't take Reagan long to move on to talking about herself anyway. She couldn't carry on a conversation without eventually directing it to herself, so Becca had merely sped up the process.

"You know that job he took at the market?"

Becca took a long sip of her coffee. "Right. As a bagger?"

"Grocery organizer."

Now it was Becca's turn to cock an eyebrow.

"All right, bagger. Well, anyway, he was laid off last night. They said he wasn't a good fit for the job."

"What happened?"

Reagan picked at her nails, took a drink of her coffee, and waved her hand through the air. "Something about smelling the fruit before he put them in the bags. He was just trying to make sure they were selling fresh produce."

"Smelling the fruit?" Becca couldn't help it; she burst out laughing, nearly falling over as she fought to keep her coffee from spilling on her laptop. "You're joking."

"Hey, it's called being nice."

Becca shook her head. "No, it's called being weird. Weird as hell, in fact. Can't you just picture him taking a big whiff of Charlotte's melons?" Then Becca realized the double meaning and broke into fresh hysterics, unable to contain herself.

"God, shut up," Reagan said, but she was smiling now, too. "You know I hate you, right? Only you would get lucky enough to score a Hamilton."

"I didn't score a Hamilton."

"Talk is you're kissing all over town . . . and doing things in his pool."

Oh, crap. She thought back to that night in the pool, but there was only woods around Nick's house. "How did they . . . never mind."

Reagan pointed at her sister now. "You are so not the good child Mama and Daddy thinks you are."

"You tell them and I'll kill you."

"My lips are sealed if you promise me one thing."

Becca waited.

"Details. All the details. Something tells me that Nick Hamilton is a lot kinkier than his glasses lets on."

Becca thought of her and Nick's time in the Keys, the things he'd done to her in bed—numerous times—and decided, yeah, he might just be.

Nick set out the ingredients he'd picked up at the market on his kitchen island. He knew Becca loved fish, and he planned to grill her the best fish of her life. Add in some fried squash and asparagus, white wine—because she liked it, even though she thought it was uppity—and French bread because the woman would eat her weight in bread if she could, and he had all the ingredients for a delicious, homemade meal. Becca's favorite kind.

The thought of taking care of her like this, treating her to something special, made him happy in a way he hadn't felt in a long time. It wasn't just about spending time with her. He wanted to show her, over and over again, how much she meant to him.

Which his brothers would probably say meant something, but while Nick was eager to shower Becca with affection, he wasn't ready to drop down on one knee, confess his love for her, and plan a spring wedding in the Square.

Still, their relationship had just begun, and he had time to figure out what he wanted and how much he could offer her. That decision didn't have to be made today.

For today, they had plans to hit the festival, or the mayor would surely hunt him down, and then come back to his house for dinner . . . and other things. Lots of other things if he hoped to top their time in the Keys. And he was more than a little excited for her to stay in his house for the first time. Though, in truth, it wasn't the first time. Or the second. Or the hundredth.

But it was the first in which they would share the same bed. And though a part of Nick wanted to delay the overnight so he could work through how he'd be with Becca in the same house where he'd been with Britt, the rest of him was eager for her to arrive. To stay as long as she was willing.

But first, they had to survive the festival.

With a quick glance outside to check the weather, Nick went to work seasoning the fish and placing it in Ziploc bags to marinate, then put everything into the fridge. He took out a beer and decided that early or not, he needed a little liquid courage. They'd gone on the weekend getaway to the Keys and they had flaunted their relationship a bit at the market, but that wasn't the same thing as holding hands in the middle of the Square and announcing to all of Triple Run that they were officially together. A couple. Exclusivity and all.

Nick wanted to protect Becca from all the extra gossip that surrounded the Hamiltons, but the problem was it had already begun. The town had separated into two sides—first there were those who felt their relationship could be disastrous for the emotional state of the town. Becca was well loved at the diner and that was the best place to get a full breakfast. Where would the trustees meet if Becca and Nick broke up?

Then there were those in town who found the whole thing romantic, the Cinderella story, the best-friends-to-lovers story, all of it right there. A Lifetime Movie played out right before them. They'd watched Nick and Becca grow up wrapped around each other, laughing and joking and getting into as much trouble as possible. And now they were kissing.

It had a Kodak moment thing to it, and nobody liked postcard moments as much as the people of Triple Run.

Nick glanced at the wall clock over his sofa, and a swirl of nervousness curled through his stomach. Wow, was he really nervous to see Becca? Becca who he'd been around several times a week since he was eight years old? Becca who'd seen him covered in chicken pox and still come over despite warnings from her parents to stay away?

Somehow that Becca and the one he wanted in his arms, in his bed, weren't the same in his mind.

This Becca was all woman, beautiful and sexy and funny and kind. He couldn't get enough of her. He never wanted this to end.

Suddenly that realization sent another flurry of uneasiness through him, but he pushed it away. They weren't making statements or promises of anything at all. They were having fun while getting to know each other in a new way.

Still, he cared about her, and a large part of him wanted to be the man for her. He wanted to take care of her, he wanted to be the man she would seek when she was afraid, the one she would seek when she was excited—the person by her side for the rest of her life.

Damn, when did that happen?

Without realizing it, he was envisioning their future.

He started down his hall, pausing at the third to last door and pressing his palm to the wood. A memory hit him of Britt decorating the space, a giant smile on her face, pages and pages of printouts around her because she could never quite get her stories the way she wanted them. She was the sort of person who was always a breath away from laughter, and Nick knew he was attracted to her as much because she brought out the good in him as anything else. Which maybe was shitty, but there it was. Still, he'd loved her. He would have married her. And they would have been happy.

Even if a part of his heart had always and would always belong to someone else.

Nick pushed away from Britt's office and into his room, continuing on to his dresser, where he pulled open the top drawer and moved aside his socks, until he found the tiny thing he was looking for—a valentine.

He could still remember when Becca gave it to him. They were ten, and he was petrified that he would be the only kid in class not to get a valentine. It ended up being a ridiculous fear because the teacher made every student send valentines to the entire class.

Still, he and Becca were out on the old tire swing behind his house, and he'd asked if she thought she'd get one, and she said yes, that Mike Campbell had a crush on her. All he could do was nod, and that was when she glanced up, caught the look on his face, and said she thought he'd for sure get one, too.

He'd found a heart valentine on his nightstand the next morning, unsure exactly how Becca had managed to get it into his room. It was a handmade, cutout heart with Nick's name on it, nothing overly fancy, but he remembered being grateful for it. For her.

Glancing at it now, Nick knew it couldn't have meant anything at all to Becca. She likely didn't remember giving it to him. But it had marked a change for Nick. That day, staring at the little heart, Becca's name written on the back, he'd realized he was no longer worried about getting a valentine from anyone else. Her heart was enough.

Now he was all too eager to get to her so he could pull her into his arms and thank her for something she'd never realized she'd done.

Becca had always accepted him for the person he was, and now, years later, Nick realized how precious that was—and how unlikely it would be for him to meet someone else who made him as happy as Becca made him.

And why should he try?

Ten minutes later, he pulled into Becca's house to pick her up for the festival. She immediately walked outside, wearing jeans and a light sweater and a smile that went straight to his heart.

"Hey, you."

"Hey, you back." Becca reached up to hug Nick, but he'd missed her too much to settle for a hug. Instead, his lips met hers, soft, enjoying the feel of them and the way her body fit perfectly against him. He felt like an idiot for not realizing it before.

Becca pouted as he pulled away. "Are you sure you want to go? We could stay and do this instead."

Nick chuckled as he kissed her cheek. "Tempting. But I'm afraid they'll just track us down if we don't show." He took her hand to lead her to his car. "Plus they'd notice, then talk, and there's enough of that already."

The air was cooler, a light breeze floating around, the smell of freshly mown grass hitting their noses as they walked. It was peaceful, perfect.

"I did something," Becca said suddenly.

"Oh?" Nick opened her car door, closed her inside, then went around to get into the driver's seat. "What did you do?"

"I applied to a college. All right, several colleges."

He turned to look at her then, shocked and excited. "Wow. Nursing?"

"Yeah. Stupid, right? I mean, I'm so far past the typical college age. And I'm not sure if my brain can handle the coursework now. It's probably harder, right? And faster-paced? With high expectations? Even if I get in, I'm going to stick out like crazy."

"You can't worry about that. It's your life, not theirs. Who cares what they think?"

"Easy for you to say." She fiddled with her seat belt and Nick reached across to steady her hands.

"Something tells me college isn't the only thing on your mind. What's up?" Nick watched Becca for her reaction, worry creeping up. She never held back like this, at least not with him.

"Bec, tell me."

"We're heading to the festival, where they all think I'm not good enough for you, and maybe they're right."

Nick pulled back. "Good enough? Wait—is that why you applied to colleges? Please tell me you're not doing this to prove something to the town. Because trust me, you're a thousand times better than me, and anyone who truly knows you knows that. I'm the lucky one here."

Her face lit up and she reached for his hand. "You're adorable when you're sweet."

"I try. But what's with the sudden interest in college?"

She stared out her window. "That one's all me, though I'd be lying if I didn't say the rest mattered to me, too. I want to measure up."

At that, Nick tugged her hand so she would face him again. "Are you kidding? To me, there's no measuring up. You've long since surpassed any benchmark I could ever reach. I'm the one who isn't good enough for you. I mean, look at me, I'd be a mess without you."

She smirked. "Well, that's true."

"You can't worry about what they think, Bec. They'll be fine. Don't you remember the gossip surrounding Trip and Emery? But they've accepted them now."

"Emery won the Derby and they have kids together."

"She's still from Crestler's Key."

Becca nodded. "I know, but the town won't be so forgiving of me. And it isn't their fault they feel that way. They like me; it isn't meant as an insult. It's just that you're royalty here—all the Hamiltons are—

and I'm the help. It's just a little unsettling now that we're . . . whatever we are."

Nick leaned over the armrest and pressed his lips to hers, gently reassuring her. "We are everything . . . to me. And I don't care about the expectation thing. My parents are long since gone, and even if they weren't, you know they wouldn't have a problem with us. They loved you. Honestly, your parents would be more likely to have a problem with me."

"That's because you set fire to Mama's roses."

"Hey, I was twelve and it was supposed to make them grow faster."

"Fire? You know how plant life works, right?"

Nick laughed. "Yeah, I was an idiot. All the more reason that you're the catch here, not me." Then he pulled her into another kiss, this one deeper, a hint of her mint bursting across his tongue. "And I have no intention of letting you go." When she finally offered him a genuine smile, he pulled out of her carport and set off toward town. "Now tell me more about the college thing."

"I applied to five and retook the SAT."

"In state?" Nick hoped his voice didn't hold the worry he felt. What would happen to them if Becca went to school in California or something, leaving him here? He would never ask her not to go, never even admit that he'd thought about it. This was big for her, and she'd already given up her dreams once. He could never ask her to do that again, especially not for him.

"Some are. Others aren't."

He nodded once. "Right, wow. I didn't even know you retook the SAT."

At that, Becca shook her head at the memory, cringing. "That was horrible. Completely horrible. Me in a room full of seventeen-year-olds. But I scored pretty well, I think. I had my scores and then my transcripts from Duke transferred, and I don't know. I still might not have a chance, but I had to try."

They parked in one of the trustee spots by Triple Run Town Hall, and Nick peered over at her again, careful to keep the worry from his expression and voice. "I'm so proud of you, you know that? First diving, then this? What else are you going to surprise me with?"

She winked playfully. "You'll have to wait until tonight for that answer."

"And what if I can't wait?" He'd leaned over to kiss her again when a knock on his window had him slowly pulling back and turning toward the offender.

"Nick?" Mayor Phillips called. "We need you." He waved to Becca. "Hello, Becca. Good to see you."

"You, too, Mayor," Becca said as she opened her car door, and then they walked around to talk to the mayor.

"What do you need, Mayor?"

"It seems some of the farm's visitors have stopped by the festival. We thought it would be nice if you, Alex, and Trip would do a photo op in front of the banner."

Nick's gaze traveled over to the large festival banner, "brought to you by Hamilton Stables" below it, and Trip and Alex already there. He hadn't spoken to them since he'd talked to William, partly because he still wasn't sure what to do but also because he didn't know if he should tell them. They were his brothers and they deserved to know the full story about the investor trying to buy Industries. He needed to tell them.

"Um, all right, but I'll need to talk to my brothers for a second first." He reached for Becca's hand, and she laced her fingers through his, only to have the mayor clear his throat. Maybe Becca was right and the town was being ridiculous about this thing. He wondered which side the mayor fell on and hoped that he would support Nick and Becca together, setting the tone for the rest of Triple Run.

It was a perfect fall day, in the low sixties, not a sign of rain. The festival featured craft stations, face painting and balloon animals for the kids, and a raffle for a fifty-inch flat screen TV. They'd run the festival for ten years now, and for the last five the streets of Triple Run had been packed, overrun with people from in town and out, there to shop for handmade goods and enjoy the food. And with a full tour schedule set to visit Hamilton Stables that day, it made sense those people would visit the festival as well.

"Hey, brother," Alex said with a grin as they approached. "Sign anything lately?"

Nick stared at his brother. "Actually, can we talk about that for a second? Privately?"

Alex eyed Trip, who motioned toward Town Hall. "It's open. We can talk in there."

"You okay?" Nick asked Becca.

"For sure. Take your time. I'll wait here."

He kissed her cheek, then followed after his brothers, his thoughts turned inward as he tried to think through what he would say without having them think this was all a ploy to change their minds.

Then he remembered the biography. He hadn't read it, but he knew Trip would have.

Once they were inside, Nick turned toward them. "I met with William Compton two weeks ago and he told me something I think you should know."

"Why didn't you tell us you were meeting with him?"

"Why didn't you tell me you were working with him in the first place?"

Trip sighed. "Point taken. What did he say?"

Swallowing hard, Nick plunged forward. "Do you remember that biography about Granddad?"

"Sure."

"Biography?" Alex asked.

"Was there mention of an affair?"

Trip's gaze leveled on him. "What's this about, Nick?"

"William said he was Dad's half brother, that Dad knew, and that Dad asked him to buy the business if it were ever in trouble. Said they made an agreement, that Dad had agreed to buy his as well."

"You're serious?"

"As a heart attack. And while I think it sounds far-fetched, I believed him. He had nothing to gain by lying."

"Only a multimillion dollar company."

"Which he could have gotten without telling us anything."

Trip stared at the floor in deep thought before finally glancing back up. "I don't think this changes anything. I'm not sure if I believe his story just yet, but I liked the man. I would feel comfortable trusting him with the business and our employees."

Nick ran a hand over his face. "If I'm honest, I liked him, too."

"So you're agreeing to sign," Alex said tentatively.

"No."

Both brothers glanced up. "Why the hell not?" Trip asked. "You said yourself you liked William. And if he's family, then that makes it an even better move."

"Maybe."

"Maybe? This has gone too far. You're forcing us into a corner, where we'll have no choice but to make this decision with or without you."

"It's my decision."

"No," Trip said, starting for the door. "It's our decision and we're done waiting."

He disappeared outside, Alex on his heels like always, and once again, Nick felt like the outsider, watching his family while he was busy trying to find a place within it.

"Nick, we need you for the picture," Mayor Phillips said from the doorway.

"Right."

"Y'all get together," the photographer from the *Tribune* said as they stood in front of the banner, all three Hamilton brothers scowling. "We'll take some photos and send them on to *Racing World* as well."

The brothers stood beside one another, Trip, Nick, then Alex, and Nick couldn't help thinking that he was surrounded by pressure—on both sides. How Trip had convinced Alex to follow him so thoroughly was beyond Nick, but he wasn't so easily swayed.

"All right, can you act a little more . . . friendly? And maybe smile?" Emery asked from nearby, a stroller and two kids with her. Kate stood right beside her with a kid entourage of her own.

"Fine," the brothers all grumbled, and it saddened Nick to realize that five years ago they would have been joking around, laughing, looking like a family. How had they allowed their differences to get between them? Business to get between them?

Though he didn't agree with Trip on the rush to sell Industries, he was still his brother, and they needed to find a way to separate the two.

Nick draped an arm around each of his brothers. "Remember that year Charlotte insisted *festival* was spelled *festavil* and had the banner reprinted and hung without anyone's approval?"

The brothers all laughed, and the photographer started snapping away.

"Or that time Patty's caught on fire?" Alex added, and they laughed still harder.

Suddenly the ridiculousness between them seemed just that—ridiculous. Couldn't they compromise? Couldn't they find a way to agree on something here, or a middle ground? But the problem was there were only two options—sell or keep Industries. There was no halfway, no gray area, and they were on opposite sides of the debate.

"Now let's do the whole family." Mayor Phillips motioned to the girls, Becca now standing with them. The mayor's eyes fell on her and he frowned. "Sorry, Becca, I think it'd be best if it were just the Hamiltons. Emery, Kate, and the kids with the brothers."

Becca's face fell for a second before she corrected herself, and Nick opened his mouth to say that Becca had been in their family longer than any of the others, but somehow the words wouldn't come out. He stared at her, across from them, and fear rippled through him.

"Becca, get in here," Emery said.

"Don't you think it would be best if the Hamilton family portrait was only Hamiltons?" the mayor asked, and several of the trustees standing nearby agreed.

Nick remained silent, a sick feeling working through him.

Becca focused on him and he looked away. "Of course. I'm going to go look around. See y'all in a bit." She turned around and disappeared into the crowd, and Nick felt like the biggest jerk imaginable. He was here with Becca; she was a longtime part of the Hamiltons. Her last name being different from the rest of them shouldn't change a thing. So why couldn't he bring himself to say any of those things?

Finally, the photo session ended, and Nick had started toward the main crowd to search for her when Trip stopped him. "What's going on with you and Becca?"

"What do you mean?" He scanned the crowd but came up empty. Surely she wouldn't leave. Though after that debacle, could he blame her?

"It's just—"

"Aren't you the one who told me I was in love with her and should be with her? And besides, what's wrong with Becca?"

"She's not the problem here. You are. Why didn't you ask her to join the photo? If you're serious about her, if she's it for you, why not have her in the family picture?" Trip stared at him and Nick stared back, his entire body numb with guilt.

He lifted an arm in Mayor Phillip's direction. "The mayor said family only."

"So? That was our photo, not the mayor's. You could have had Patty in it for all it mattered. So why did you let the mayor make Becca feel like she's not as important to you as Emery is to me, Kate to Alex?"

"Emery's your wife and Kate is Alex's wife. Becca's not my wife."

"But she could be, and she's definitely been in and around our family long enough to be in that picture. But you didn't want her there. Just like you have no intention of marrying her, and that's not fair to her. This, whatever the hell it is you're doing, isn't fair to her. It's selfish, just like this shit with Industries, and it's time you put the rest of us before yourself."

Nick opened his mouth to speak, but once again, no words came out. He glanced around as if for help, but there was no way out of this. No one to support his stupidity. Because Trip was right.

"Yeah, that's what I thought. Pull yourself together, man. Before you wreck the best thing that's ever happened to you." Trip walked away, leaving Nick standing there, unable to move or speak or think. What the hell was he thinking during that photo session?

He wasn't.

The mayor had called out the very thing Becca was worried about, and Nick had let him. He owed her an apology, but how could he apologize without revealing the deeper issues there? At the end of the day, when it was all said and done, he wasn't sure about their future. Not really. He cared for Becca, more than he'd ever cared about anyone, including Britt, yet he knew he wouldn't propose.

The pain of losing Becca would destroy him, put the final nail in his coffin. It was basic human instinct to protect oneself from harm, and that was what Nick was doing.

So why had he even started this with Becca? What was the plan or purpose there? Hell if there was one, and now he'd hurt the one person he cared about most.

Damn it all to hell.

He had to find her, and fast, before she figured out what Trip had, and ended things with Nick for good.

Chapter Fourteen

Becca's chest hurt and her cheeks were still so prickly from the humiliation of it all that she worried the red might never disappear.

Just like the ache in her heart.

Only the Hamiltons.

Right. And she wasn't a Hamilton. She would never, ever be a Hamilton. But why didn't Nick say something? Defend her? Why didn't he shout out that it didn't matter if she was a Hamilton, she was with him?

And that was when Becca realized the truth—Nick might care about her but he didn't love her. Not the way she wanted to be loved and not the way she loved him.

What in the hell was she thinking, getting involved with Nick? There were some crushes that were never meant to be realized. Sort of like that obsession she'd had with Johnny Depp during the *Pirates of the Caribbean* years. There was no happily ever after for her and Johnny. And there was no happily ever after for her and Nick. Only where the Johnny thing had been easy to shrug off—after all, Johnny Depp didn't exactly live a few doors away—Nick wasn't so easy to dismiss.

The pain in her heart, coupled with the kind of humiliation that one should never have to face, weighed so heavily on her that she needed to find a quick place to hide before the whole town saw the truth. She loved him . . . and he didn't love her back.

And there was the real problem—she didn't just care for Nick. She loved him. Good God, she loved him. So much that she'd never once stopped to think whether she *should* love him, whether it was worth risking her dignity and self-respect to be with him. Because while she might just be Triple Run's waitress of the year, she did have a place in the town. People waved and smiled at her, they appreciated her role in making the town function.

Now she was just the stupid woman who'd blindly thought she could have a future with a man who'd buried his future years ago. She was an idiot.

Needing a break from the stares and a place to hide until she could control her emotions, she disappeared inside Triple Run Recruiting to visit Priscilla.

"Hey, honey," Priscilla said with jubilance as she came out of her office. "I'd have thought you'd be out there enjoying the festivities with that fine man of yours."

Becca felt tears bubbling up and tried her best to swallow them back. She wasn't a crier, and the idea of doing it now, something half the town already knew would happen, made her feel like a stupid woman. Though maybe she *was* a stupid woman.

"But see, that's the thing. I don't think he is mine. Not really. I don't think he'll ever be mine. And I don't know what to make of that. I don't know how to continue on if there's only a wall before me."

She drew a rattled breath, blinking back tears that refused to stop. "You must think I'm crazy, coming here talking all this nonsense. I just . . . well, I don't have anybody else. My sister's ridiculous and my mama and daddy live out of state, and the only real family I have here are the Hamiltons, though, apparently, that was all just in my head, and now . . ." Tears rained down and she was unable to stop them, a lifetime of pent-up hurt spilling over, and Becca wondered when exactly she became this mess of a woman. Her bottom lip trembled as she peered back up at Priscilla. "I'm sorry."

"Aw, honey, we all need a good cry sometimes, and I'm more than happy to be the one to hear it. You come here whenever you like. I actually don't have anybody either, so maybe we could be there for each other. How's that sound?"

Becca nodded slowly, a fresh sob starting, and Priscilla started for her, just as the shop's door opened and Priscilla's gaze swung over, then back to Becca.

"There you are. I've been looking everywhere for you, and Charlotte said she thought you came in here, and I said no, but then . . ." Nick trailed off, and Becca tried frantically to clean up her face with her shirt sleeve. "Bec . . ."

Sure she had no choice, she turned slowly and smiled weakly. "Well, you found me." Her voice broke right along with her heart, and the devilish tears refused to stop their evil reign over her face.

"I'm such an asshole."

"I'll second that," Priscilla said, "but I'll give you two a minute." She stepped around Nick, patting his shoulder, and then disappeared out of her shop.

Immediately, Nick started for her. "I'm so sorry. I don't know what to say. I don't know why I didn't step in and tell the mayor to screw himself, that you were my family and belonged in that picture. That it didn't matter what your last name was, that you've been a Hamilton since the moment I met you. I just . . ."

"Didn't." Becca worked to wipe away the tears, but they refused to stop. She was a soaked mess now, her throat thick from crying, her eyes puffy, her nose running away. "Dammit." She walked over and grabbed a tissue from Priscilla's desk. "I don't do this."

"I know."

"You made me do this."

"I know that, too."

Becca stopped to look at him and the pang in her chest worsened. She thought of all their years around each other, all the jokes and pranks and fun, only to end up here. The joke was on her. "No, I'm wrong. It wasn't you, it's me."

Nick waved his hands. "No, no, it's definitely me. One hundred and fifty percent me. I just don't know how to fix it. Just . . . can you not leave? Can you give me a chance to fix myself? To be what you need? I know I'm not a whole man anymore, that I'm some ghost of a person, but I want to be more. For you, I want to be more. Just please . . . can we try?" He edged closer to her, and though she wanted to step away, to protect her heart from this man who'd owned it since she was old enough to give it away, she couldn't. Because hearts didn't work that way, and love never had understood good sense.

Tentatively, Nick reached out for her hand and she let him, more because she needed to feel like there was hope than anything else, and though that made her as weak as they came, there it was. She had never claimed to be strong about Nick anyway.

"I'm sorry," Nick repeated. "Unbelievably sorry."

"I know."

He ran a hand over her cheek, catching a tear. "This is only the third time I've ever seen you cry. The first was when your grand-mother died, and now twice I've caused you tears."

Becca shrugged, not wanting to talk about the crying or what it meant. For now, she just wanted to feel better. The rest could be dealt with tomorrow, when her emotions weren't all over the place and she could think properly.

Only would a day change anything? She would still love him and he would still refuse to love her back.

"I think I should go home. Alone."

"Can we go back to my place instead? Talk? You can throw things at me if you'd like. I had plans to make you the best dinner of your life."

"The throwing thing is tempting." She hesitated. "The best dinner of my life, huh?" Becca tried to smile, though she couldn't quite make it work. She was still so sad and embarrassed. She had no idea what would fix the hurt in her chest, but pushing Nick away certainly wouldn't. "I am kind of hungry."

Nick kissed her temple and held her close. "I'll fix this. With the town and with you. Please don't give up on us yet."

"Okay."

"Okay." Nick took her hand and they walked out of Priscilla's. There were so many people that while she felt sure some were watching them, most were busy with their own lives. Laughing with their kids, buying goodies, living. And despite whatever happened between her and Nick, it was time for her to live, too.

For the first time, she was glad she'd applied to the colleges. They might all say no, but at least she was trying—living.

It took a surprisingly short amount of time to make it to Nick's house, considering neither of them spoke. Becca stayed focused out her window, and the few times she glanced over at Nick, she'd catch worry lines creasing his face before he'd smile at her, putting on a show.

She wanted to ask what was really going on in his head, but for once she was scared to know. Confirmation of all the things she feared could break her completely, and right now she just wanted to enjoy their time together. As short as it might be.

Nick opened her car door and they walked on into his house.

"I'll get dinner going."

Becca nodded. "Is it okay if I use the bathroom? You know, get cleaned up?"

"You've never asked before."

Becca stared at him. He was right. Never once had she felt so uneasy in his house, so out of her element. Normally, she came and went as she pleased, but her skin felt too thin and her heart too heavy, and she didn't know how to be right now, feeling like such a shell of a person.

"Right," she finally said, unsure of what else to say, and then she disappeared down the hall, glad to be away from Nick for a moment so she could think. And that's when her gaze landed on Britt's office, the door closed. She knew she should continue on to the next door, the bathroom, but she couldn't seem to make her feet work.

It had been years since she'd been in that room and she could scarcely remember what it looked like, but Becca wondered if Nick had left it untouched. Had he cleaned out the room and turned it into something else, a small workout room or something? Or was he holding on to his dead fiancée by keeping the room exactly as it had been? That singular difference would let her know if they had a chance or if he would always be tied to a ghost.

She had to know.

Peering back down the hall, she listened to the sound of Nick rummaging around in the kitchen. This was wrong—so, so wrong. But she couldn't walk past this room after what had just happened at the festival without checking. After all, there had been photos of the family at the festival back then, too, and Britt had been in them. She and Nick weren't married yet, she wasn't yet a Hamilton, and yet he'd openly asked her to join the family photo.

Which was maybe what made it sting that much more that Becca hadn't been included. Britt had been his family, even before they were legally bound, so why not Becca?

Her hand found its way to the doorknob even as she scolded herself over and over, ordering herself to walk away, be the good girl she'd always been, but she was tired of being that girl. That *woman*, because honestly, it'd been a long time since she was a girl, and yet she didn't feel like she'd experienced the trials and tribulations of life that turned a girl into a woman.

"Do or die." And then she cracked the door open. With one more glance down the hall, she stepped inside the room, her heart pounding in her chest, her pulse in her ears, her eyes burning.

Because the room was exactly as she remembered it, not a single thing moved, like a fossil perfectly preserved within Nick's house.

The back wall was all windows cradled in plaid drapes. Against the left wall stood floor-to-ceiling shelves, slap full of every book imaginable. Britt's wide black desk sat against the right wall, a leather armchair in front of it, an ivory throw tossed over the chair.

Becca pictured Britt in there working, the throw draped around her shoulders, a cup of coffee on her desk, the day just beginning. Birds would sing outside her window, the air would be cool, that smile she wore like a favorite sweater would forever rest on her face. Even in the earliest parts of the day, when nobody smiled, Britt would smile. No wonder he'd loved her so much.

God, what was she doing in there?

Fresh tears filled her eyes and she reached out to steady herself, only to knock the throw to the floor. Frantically she reached down for it, praying she hadn't gotten it dirty, just as she heard the hinges on the office door whine and then— "What are you doing in here?" And then a sharp intake of breath and fast footsteps as he reached down and took the throw from Becca's hands. "What did you do?" He fought to put the throw back over the chair in the exact way it had been before.

"I didn't mean to. I was reaching for the chair and knocked it over. I—"

"You shouldn't be in here at all."

At the cold tone in his voice, Becca's eyes began to water again, but she wouldn't cry. Not now. Pushing away the hurt, she took a step away from the man she loved. "Take me home." There was a lot Becca could take, but being treated like this wasn't one of them. She had been there for Nick through everything, and if her walking into Britt's old office and accidentally knocking something over was enough for him to look at her like that, talk to her like that, then she was done.

Nick's gaze jerked from the throw to Becca, the rage quickly replaced with horror, then fear, and finally sadness. "Bec, I shouldn't have . . . I don't know why I—"

"Take me home!"

Nick flinched, but then his shoulders slumped and he nodded in defeat. "I'll grab my keys."

Chapter Fifteen

"Come on, Bec, answer. Please answer." Nick's cell rang away, his hand tight around it like it could somehow fix this situation. But there was no fixing this. No, he had royally screwed up. No flowers, no chocolate, no apology could undo this mess.

It had been a week since the incident in Britt's office, and still, he couldn't figure out what had happened. Why he'd reacted that way.

Not only had he overreacted but he'd treated Becca like she was a stranger, an enemy—there to mess up Britt's perfect room. And why had he kept her office so pristine anyway? Who cared? Britt would have made fun of him if she were still alive, accused him of being a hoarder, of staying still instead of moving forward. And she would be right. But every time Nick tried to go into the room, he'd freeze and back out, unable to face all those emotions. Like he was a fragile twig in an ice storm, just trying to keep from breaking.

Still, he'd told himself he would keep all of that separate from Becca, who had been his savior over the years. Time and time again she'd proven to be the only light leading him home. She was brightness to Britt's death's darkness, and when the two worlds collided, he hadn't known how to deal.

But how could he explain that he wasn't trying to hurt her, that he didn't mean to make her feel like an outsider in his life?

He couldn't.

Because actions and perceptions were reality, and there was no talking his way out of this horror.

Becca's voice from her voice mail greeting filled the void, sweet and Southern to the core, and his heart twisted a bit tighter. "Bec, it's me. Again. I am so sorry. I don't know what overcame me. I don't know what I was thinking. I just . . . please call me."

He hung up and started into the office, pissed at the world. It wasn't until he exited onto the floor and started through the doors that he realized something wasn't right. The floor was eerily quiet, everyone too focused on their work. His gaze went immediately to his assistant, and she pointed to the conference room, then immediately ducked back into her chair and hid behind her computer.

Nick's eyes went to the lit conference room, the men in suits around the table, and all he could see was red.

The whole place became a betrayal. The staff for not warning him when he walked in, the smell of coffee in the air, as though everything were normal. As though his brothers weren't meeting there right this second to sell the place. Again without telling him. He wondered how it was possible to feel such anger without spontaneously combusting.

But instead of walking into the conference room and throwing chairs like he wanted to, he walked over to the doorway and peered inside, watching in silence as his brothers interacted with Compton and his team. The smiles on their faces. The genuine laughs. Like a family.

When was the last time Nick had laughed so freely here, smiled and enjoyed his job? Months . . . years.

He thought of what Trip had said before, about Nick hanging on for his own interest while making life miserable for everyone else there, and as he peered around the office, he tried to remember what it used to be like there. What sounds should he hear now?

Conversation, some about work, others about their kids' latest Little League game. Because Hamilton Industries had always been the kind of place that supported a work-life balance. But as he took in his staff, he realized they weren't talking.

No, they were focused on their computer screens, their backs hunched over, their arms tense as their fingers worked away at the keyboards.

They were miserable, every last one of them. Miserable. When had that happened? And maybe, as importantly for his current state of being, had he caused it?

He thought of the person he'd been since his father died, his refusal to release anything, a finger on every aspect of the business, and realized he had his answer. Not only had he caused their misery, he'd facilitated it. He'd helped it grow.

All for what?

Nick himself was miserable. He had no friends, he was barely speaking to his brothers, and he'd hurt the one person who could make all the rest seem unimportant.

He thought of going into the conference room, signing away the company, his life, but he was too unstable right now, and the last thing he wanted to do was make an emotional decision he couldn't undo.

So instead of walking in, announcing his arrival, and hashing it out with his brothers, he turned on his heel and walked out.

At first, he thought of going to Becca's and begging her to forgive him, if only for today so he could feel a bit of relief. But at his core, he wasn't the selfish ass he'd been these last few years, and he couldn't be that person with her. With anyone else, but not with her.

Which left only one place.

Nick slid back into his car, slower than he'd left it, and started driving. He thought of his life, all the people in it. What did he want? At the end of the day, opinions aside, judgment from others aside, what did he want?

He wanted Becca.

He wanted his family back together.

He wanted to contribute to the family business.

He wanted to marry and have kids. Though it scared him, he wanted those things.

But how could he make those things a reality after all he'd done to destroy them?

He drove on, disappearing down back road after back road, driving and thinking and driving some more, until he found himself at the one place that might help.

Nick slowed down as he pulled into the memorial park, his heart picking up speed though his car was barely inching along. As if on a string, he continued around the turns, right, left, right, left, until he could see the large headstone, a bronze Thoroughbred at the top, and parked his car.

It took a solid minute to muster the courage to get out of the car, but once he did, and took in the dead flowers on his father's grave, he cursed himself for not being a better son, even in death. He had let his fears and sadness control him until he was no longer a strong Hamilton, like Trip and Alex. He should have tried harder. In every part of his life, he should have been stronger.

The morning air was still crisp, a hint of a storm brewing overhead, and Nick thought how fitting it would be if it rained today. Maybe then he could melt away and let his feelings overwhelm him like he craved. But he was done avoiding things. Which was why he was here. He needed to explain, and then, once he was done, he needed to ask for forgiveness.

"Hey, Dad, it's me," Nick said as he hovered above the grave, reading each line etched into the headstone as though he didn't already know the words by heart.

Carter Hamilton
A good husband, a great father, and an even better friend.
You will be missed.

He read the words again and thought of the day he'd chosen them, how he'd shown them to Alex and Trip, how they'd nodded along as though it weren't a big deal, when it was everything. And maybe that was part of the animosity he felt toward his brothers now.

Nick had been there, planning every element of their father's funeral even before he was dead, and never once had they said thanks. Had they said they were sorry he carried the burden alone. Never had they said anything at all.

He resented them. Every single thing about them. Their solidity in their careers. Their beautiful wives and stables' worth of kids. Their lives, so perfectly put together, while his was slowly but surely falling apart.

But that wasn't fair. They deserved to be happy, had earned that happiness, and he was a jerk for wishing anything less for them.

He ran his hands through his hair and knelt in the grass. Still wet from yesterday's rain, it soaked through his khakis to his skin, but he remained kneeling.

"I know about William. I'm not sure why you didn't tell us, but I know. Trip and Alex know, too. And we've made the decision to sell Hamilton Industries. I tried to . . ." He paused, drew a long breath, and started again. "No, I didn't try. I let it go. I tried to micromanage everything, when what I needed to do was pull back and let business do what it did. Instead, I tried over and over to shove a square through a circular hole, and it didn't work. To be honest, I should have sold a year ago, but I couldn't. I just . . . I didn't want to disappoint you, and yet I've done that anyway. And I'm sorry. God, I'm sorry. I have never felt sorrier in my life than I feel right now, and not just for disappointing you. I've disappointed everyone. And I'm sorry for that, for so many things. And I would come here every day and say it all over again if I thought it would do any good, but it won't. We still have to sell and it's my fault, and nothing I say today and nothing I could do tomorrow could change it."

His head dropped, the pain so real he thought he might never stand back up. "I'm sorry I couldn't be the man you raised me to be. And I've screwed everything else up in my life, too. Trip and Alex hate me, and I've pushed away the woman I love. All for what? Fear? Doubt? I don't know when I started second-guessing everything in my life, but I'm tired of it. I might never be able to fix anything, but I'm not willing to let fear define me anymore."

Unable to stay there any longer, he pushed to standing and started for his car, only to spy another one behind his, and a pretty brunette outside it, leaning against the door.

"You okay?" Becca asked, her tone caring yet impersonal. The kind of question the nurse at a doctor's office might ask you, before going on to ask every unconscionable question under the sun.

"Not really." It was the most honest thing Nick had ever said. "What are you doing here?"

"Your brothers said they saw you at the office."

"Trip called you?"

"Actually, it was Alex," she said, fiddling with her shirt. "What are you doing here?"

"Did I tell you that my dad had a half brother? That he was the one trying to buy Industries?"

"No, but that's great, though, right?"

Nick tilted his head up so he could see her more clearly. "Is it?"

"It's family. More is almost always better. Well, unless you're a Stark; then it's questionable." She smiled, but it didn't reach her eyes the way a true Becca smile would have. The pang in his heart deepened.

"We decided to sell." Nick laughed sarcastically. "No, they decided to sell."

Becca nodded. "I guess it's their decision to make."

"What? Not you, too?"

Her eyes lifted to his, a hint of challenge within them. "I said it was their decision to make. And it is."

"Their decision? They didn't help build that company."

"Neither did you."

Nick's face filled with anger and hurt. "You know I did. You know I worked my ass off there for years."

"Yes, but your father and grandfather built the business, and Carter left it to all three of you. It's a family decision, and you were cutting them out of it. Forcing them to lose the only chance you might have of selling it. That isn't right."

"What's not right is them selling their shares behind my back, without telling me, forcing me to sell, too, or else piss off the whole company. This was Dad's company! How could they want to sell it?"

Becca edged closer now, the anger in her eyes softening, but Nick was already too far gone.

"They did tell you. They've been telling you for weeks and months now, and Trip's a smart businessman. He wouldn't agree to sell if it weren't the right decision."

"Right, because he's such a better businessman than me, right? His part of the company is still thriving, while we're forced to sell mine."

Becca closed her eyes briefly, like she was drawing up the patience a mother needed to deal with her two-year-old in the middle of a tantrum. "That's not what I said."

"That's what you meant, right? That's what everyone's saying here. And then what? They expect me to go work at Stables, under Trip, like everyone else? Screw that."

"You wouldn't work under him. You would all three run it together. Why are you being a baby about this? Yes, I said it. You're being a baby. Businesses are bought and sold every day. That doesn't make you a failure."

Nick stared at the woman before him, sure that what she was saying was true, but he couldn't bring himself to believe it. He'd hit rock bottom, nowhere to go but to swim in his own misery, and she deserved better. It was time he did the right things in his life—with his brothers . . . and with Becca. "I can't do this."

Becca's gaze flicked over from Carter's grave to Nick. "What?"

"This; you and me. I was never the right man for you. This whole thing makes that abundantly clear. I'm not the man for anyone right now. I've got personal shit stacked up to the sky and no idea how to tackle any of it. I'm a mess and I don't know how to clean it up. I'm not bringing you down with me. I care about you too much."

Becca turned to get in her car and paused at the door. "You know, screw that. I came here as your friend. Us, you and me, whatever we were, was over the moment you treated me like an intruder in your home the other night. *I* ended this. Don't mistake that. Me, not you. Which maybe seems trivial to you, but it matters to me. Still, you were my best friend and Alex called, and I knew you must be hurting, so I came. And yet again, you've tossed me to the ground. I'm over it. I can't be around you anymore. You're toxic, and I just . . . *I* can't do this anymore."

She slipped into her Highlander and drove away, leaving Nick staring after her, sure that he'd ruined the only good thing in his life. But his misery didn't need company, and in the end, he was doing her a favor.

Twenty-plus years of friendship . . . gone.

Now Nick had lost everything.

Chapter Sixteen

Becca stopped at her mailbox and pulled out all the envelopes and retail mailers inside, her heart so heavy it could have weighed down the whole car, the whole world. How had things gone from good to bad so quickly?

Rain had set in and thunder boomed overhead, matching her mood, and for once she was glad she lived alone. She didn't want to explain to anyone what had happened with Nick, especially when she couldn't really explain it to herself.

The great problem was that Becca was never Nick's first choice. His first choice died years ago, and she would forever be a ghost of a version of Britt. Becca might be the person who could fill the space for a bit, but she would never perfectly conform.

And while she loved Nick, so much so that she'd gone to the grave today despite her lovesick heart, she wouldn't survive a relationship with him. Her ego, her heart, her sanity couldn't survive it. She would forever be trying to measure up and failing at every turn.

Becca dropped the mail on the kitchen counter and went on to her room to put on some warm clothes. Once she was in her flannel PJs and fluffy socks, she padded back into the kitchen, just as a knock sounded on the door.

A part of her hoped it would be Nick, on his knees, begging her to forgive him. But an apology wouldn't fix this, and besides, he'd made his decision. He was over it, over her.

Sadness took hold of her again, until she peered down at the giant box on her front porch, Walmart printed on the outside, and she squealed with excitement. She might not have Nick or a fancy job or an acceptance to a college. But she did have a Keurig.

She went to work tearing open the Walmart box, then the Keurig box, until she finally had it out and on her counter in all its shiny black wonder. Wrapping her arms around it, she hugged it close. "Thank God for coffee." Then she followed the instructions to clean it and finally had it all set up beside her refrigerator, the other one still there like a tube TV beside a flat screen.

"Sorry to do this, but you're out of here." She threw the old one in the trash and grinned at her new fancy coffeemaker, reminding herself that in life it was the little things that mattered, and whatever those little things were, you should hold on to them. Appreciate them. And right now, her little thing was a Keurig coffeemaker.

She turned it on and placed a K-Cup inside, started the coffee, and then grabbed the mail. Flipping through each envelope, she sorted them into bills to pay or junk, and that was when her fingers latched onto the next to the last envelope.

Vanderbilt University.

Her heart heaved as she peered down at the envelope. "Oh my God."

It was a large envelope, but it was thin. Too thin for anything awesome to be inside. But maybe everything was online now and the letter just read that she was accepted and directed her where to go online to look for the rest. That could happen. Maybe.

Stop being a chicken and open it, she told herself. She decided to grab her coffee instead, sure she needed a little liquid courage, and in Becca's world, that liquid was coffee.

Finally, she had her coffee in hand and no more excuses.

With a deep breath, she slowly tore the top of the envelope inch by inch. Snails moved at a faster pace, but she was too nervous and excited to go fast. Once the envelope was open, she slid out the letter inside, closed her eyes to say a quick prayer, then reopened them and looked down, only to read the words, "Dear Ms. Stark, Thank you for your interest in Vanderbilt University. We are sorry to inform you . . ."

She didn't get in. And they were sorry, which was just another way of saying she wasn't good enough.

She thought of her application, and how silly she was to think she could go back to school after all these years and compete with kids coming out of school with a wealth of extracurricular activities and studies tailored specifically for college. They spent four years preparing for college, and she'd naively thought one afternoon of applying would be enough.

And now for the rest of her life she'd work at that diner, pouring drinks and bringing out food, and for the right person that would be fine. There was no dishonor in working hard and earning a living, however you did it, but Becca wanted more. And then, to add salt to the wound, she'd have to listen to the town talk about how she and Nick broke up, how it was a shame but expected. And she'd have to face running into Nick and the Hamiltons there and all over town, knowing what had happened between them. How could she face everyone who already thought she wasn't good enough and confirm that they were right—she wasn't.

God, what was she going to do?

She made another cup of coffee, though this one didn't bring her the happiness of the first, and sat down on the couch, eager to find a fix, but there was nothing in sight, no hope here.

Sadness overwhelmed her and she pulled the throw off the back of the couch and placed it over her legs, but then she thought of that ivory throw in Britt's office and Nick's reaction, and Becca threw the blanket across the room. A sob broke free and she lay down, thinking of how stupid she'd been, and how much she wished she could turn back time.

If only she could turn back time. She would keep her feelings to herself and try to find a way to move on, meet a good man and dedicate herself to loving him, put aside her silly childhood crush. But how could you make yourself stop loving someone? How could you repair the hole in your heart at learning he didn't love you back?

A fresh sob worked through her body, and though she hated crying, she knew she wouldn't be able to stop it. So she curled up without a blanket, without a college acceptance letter . . . and without Nick.

"Order up, Becca." Sage eyed her, sadness creasing the lines around his eyes, and Becca wished she could hug the old man for caring so much.

News had circulated through Triple Run—the Cinderella story was over. A Stark would not be marrying a Hamilton. Half the town was thrilled, the other sad that fairy tales weren't a reality, at least not in Triple Run, or maybe just not for Becca.

"Thanks." She grabbed the plates and started away as Sage reached out to stop her.

"You okay?"

Becca bit her lip and tried to look at him, but she couldn't quite make her eyes lift. Her mama always said time would heal any hurting, and if that didn't work, try some wine. Well, Becca was ready to toss in her coffee for a wine habit just to see if it would help. Only she had never been a pleasant drunk and she hated headaches, so the wine thing might not suit her after all. "I will be."

"You let me know if anyone gives you trouble." The cook's eyes fell on the trustee table in the center of the diner, one seat empty. "I put Willow on that table."

"Thank you."

Becca started away just as Sage's rough voice spoke again. "Don't let them make you feel inferior. We might not have wealth, but that doesn't make us less than them. The Hamiltons have long been royalty here, but that doesn't mean they rule us. You are just as important as them, and you deserve a man who knows what he has."

She nodded to him, unable to form words and thankful for the first time that she'd cried so hard the day before, because maybe now she was all cried out and could survive this day without embarrassing herself.

"All right, then; take that before it burns your hand."

Becca set down the plates at the first table and continued on around the diner, setting down plates, faking smiles, trying her very best not to be the dark cloud in the restaurant, bringing everyone else down with her depression. But the truth was she was sad in a way she never thought possible, and it wasn't just because of Nick. It was the realization that all her dreams were just that—dreams. Silly, ridiculous dreams that would never be a reality.

Needing a moment, she motioned to Sage that she was going on her nonsmoker break and stepped outside.

"Becca!"

What now? Becca spun around to see who had called for her at the same time Reagan ran up to her.

"There you are!"

For a second, fear replaced Becca's sadness. "Are you okay? Are the kids?"

Reagan waved her off. "Yeah, yeah. It's not me. It's you. Look what was delivered to my house by mistake! Look! It's huge and thick and has to mean you were accepted." She passed Becca a large envelope, the words *University of Kentucky* printed across the front.

Becca's eyes widered as she looked down at it and then up at her sister. Reagan was right—the envelope was huge and bulky. But Becca had already been through this once, and she was afraid her fragile heart couldn't take any more breaking. She passed it back to her sister. "Can you put it on my counter? I can't open it right now."

"Why?"

"What if it's a no? I mean, surely it's a no, right?"

"They don't send nos in giant envelopes like this. Open it." Reagan tried to put the envelope back in Becca's hands, but she stepped away, waving her off.

"I can't."

"Fine, if you won't open it, I'll open it for you." Reagan ripped open the envelope and pulled out the contents, a smile forming as she read the letter. Happiness took over her face as she focused back on Becca. "They said yes. You're in!" She jumped up and down and handed the letter over to Becca, who was sure her sister was joking. Surely she was joking.

But then Becca scanned the letter, tears pricking her eyes as she read. Apparently, her eyes were still open to happy tears, because she was in. Accepted. "We're pleased to inform you that you've been accepted to the College of Nursing."

"Oh my God."

"I know! You're going to be a nurse!"

The letter rattled in Becca's hands, and she realized she was shaking, excitement moving through her, a rush unlike anything she'd felt before. The rush of accomplishment, the rush of success, the rush of something finally going right.

"I'm going to be a nurse."

Chapter Seventeen

The world had somehow turned dark overnight, but Nick told himself he had bounced back from misery before and he could do it again. Honestly, he should be an expert by now, but this was different. He felt like his body had been broken in half and he didn't know how to function without the other side, how to walk around or breathe. How to be.

He felt like a fool to think he could cut Becca out of his life without suffering the greatest loss of his lifetime; this was so much worse than every bad thing he'd experienced before it.

Becca wasn't just a friend or family—she was his match, the person put on this Earth for him, and he was put here for her, and his job was to protect her and keep her safe. And instead he'd devastated her with blow after blow.

It had been two weeks, and a part of him wanted to call her and apologize, beg her to forgive him, offer her anything in the world to make her agree. But then he'd remember all the reasons he'd pushed her away in the first place, that he wasn't where he needed to be for a relationship, that she deserved better, that until his life was in order he couldn't guarantee the quality of person he would be each day.

She deserved much, much more than a disgruntled version of Nick Hamilton, and lately that was all he could offer.

An ad for Hamilton Stables flashed across the TV, and Nick watched as the camera showed the beauty of the farm, the advancements, an aerial shot of the full staff, hundreds of people dedicated to the farm, and then the declaration that it was a family-owned business.

Family-owned.

Family.

And he was part of that family. He'd allowed his pride to stand in the way, but he was a Hamilton. He couldn't remember how or why he'd separated himself from his family. When did he decide that it was more important to care for his father's memory than to continue the legacy of a family that worked as a family—together?

It was time for a change.

Pushing off his couch, he went to his room, threw on some jeans and a pullover, his boots, and headed out the door, sure of something for the first time in a long time.

He was done being the reason his family wasn't together.

The air was cold as it blew past him in the golf cart. It had been a long time since he'd driven it around the farm, and as he took in the scenery, he was proud of what Trip and Alex had done there. They deserved praise for their work, and maybe, just maybe, he could be a part of all this again.

The main office was busier than usual, people milling all around, and Nick hoped Trip was in his office and not out of town or at the track.

Ignoring the curious glances from the staff, Nick continued on down the main hall and knocked on the last door at the end, a small lump forming in his throat as he thought of Carter in that same office. But that legacy was over, and it was time to build a new one.

"Come on in," Trip called, but as Nick edged inside, his expression said he wished he'd ignored the knock. "Nick."

"Can we talk?"

"You said a lot the last time we spoke. Words like *asshole* and *traitor* come to mind."

Nick flinched at the memory of him calling Trip after leaving the grave. "I'm sorry about that."

"What was that? I don't understand. You like William, we've proven that he's telling the truth, he was Dad's half brother. You know business is declining. Why are you making things so hard?"

With effort, Nick continued on into the office. His ego had no place in this meeting and he refused to let it come into play now. "I don't know, but I'm sorry. For not listening to you, for not seeing what was obvious, for knowing the right decision to make but refusing to make it."

Trip eyed his brother, then clicked his phone, and, "Hamilton," filled the air. "Hey, it's me. Nick's here. Can you come over?"

"Yep," Alex said. "Be there in a sec."

A door closed out in the hall, and then Trip's door opened and Alex stepped in, an uneasy expression on his face. "Are we entering another yelling match? 'Cause if so, I'd like to grab my earbuds." Even with the tension, he was smiling, never one to hold a grudge.

"No yelling," Nick said, releasing a long breath. "I actually came to say I'm sorry. And that y'all were right. I was wrong."

"Does that mean you're agreeing to sell?"

Nick licked his lips and considered the option one more time, but the truth was, his family was more important than Industries. Than the farm. Than any of it. He refused to be the reason they weren't talking. And besides, the numbers spoke for themselves. He'd talked with the controller, ran over the numbers again himself. This was the right decision, and the business and staff would be safe under William's control. "Yes," Nick said finally. "I'll sign. I care more about our family than I do the legacy of what Dad created. I wanted to protect his work, but I was destroying it in the process. And destroying our relationship. I'm sorry for that. So yes, I'll sign, but under one condition."

Trip straightened, readying for another argument. "What's that?"

"I work in the offices here. I don't want to walk away from the family business. I want to help; whatever that is, I'll do it."

Trip eyed Alex and then sighed loudly, and Nick feared he'd ruined their relationship, taken things too far, said too much. Then a wide smile took over Trip's face. "We thought we'd have to convince you to come here. Alex had a plan all in place."

Alex grinned. "It may or may not have involved blackmail."

A laugh broke free from Nick this time. "The trophy bass?"

"You know it. I caught that fish, and you were put on the cover of the damn magazine and given all those endorsements. That should have been me."

"Still saying that, huh?"

"It was my setup that caught it."

Nick laughed again. "In my hands."

"Whatever." Then the brothers all glanced at one another, the moment easier.

"We'd be lucky to have you," Trip said. "Alex is slammed with breeding and the training schedule has me traveling more these days. We need someone managing the business, all of it. The financials, keeping us on track. Double-checking the whole staff to make sure they have what they need. Setting tour dates. And no one would do a better job than you."

"I would love that. But I can also clean stalls, if that's what you want." At that, his brothers burst into laughter. "All right, fine. Maybe not the stalls thing."

"That's what we thought, Ivy League boy. But we'll put that brain of yours to good use, and you'll likely have us in shape in no time. I'll warn you, it's a beast."

"Put me in, Coach."

Trip reached out to shake Nick's hand, then pulled him into a hug instead. "I've missed you."

"Me too," Alex said, patting his back. "Glad to have you back."

Nick swallowed hard. "Glad to be back. Now, not to flake on the first day, but I've got to head out."

"What?" the brothers said together.

"Gotta go see about a girl." It was the same thing he'd said to Mama V what felt like ages ago, but this time there was no doubt in his mind of what he wanted and he would do anything to get her.

"Becca?" Nick searched frantically inside her house, not bothering to knock, though in hindsight he probably should have. It wasn't like they were on the best of terms right now, but old habits died hard.

"She's not here," a voice called from the kitchen, and Nick peered over to see Reagan there, making coffee. Nick's gaze went to the coffeemaker beside her.

"She bought a Keurig?"

"Yep." Reagan took a long sip, her gaze cold and her demeanor clear. She was dressed in head-to-toe black, which fit the glare she shot at Nick perfectly. "She's not here."

Nick motioned outside. "Her Highlander is in the carport."

"She took Uncle Mark's truck."

"Took it where?" Suddenly, Nick got the feeling he was missing something important, and as he peered around the house, he realized there were things missing. Lots of things. And boxes, some full, others waiting to be filled. "What is all this?"

"She was accepted to the University of Kentucky's nursing program. She's moving to Lexington. Actually, she's already there. She took the truck so she could pack in more boxes. She's going to be a nurse."

At that Nick's gaze snapped over to Reagan. "She got in." He couldn't keep the smile from his voice. She'd done it, her dream; she was going to be a nurse.

"No thanks to you."

That stung, but Nick knew he deserved it. "You're right. I screwed up. But I want to fix it. I was . . . it doesn't even matter why. There's no excuse, but I love her, Reagan. And I'm hoping she loves me enough to forgive me. And then I'll spend the rest of my life making this up to her, because she's everything to me. Please, I've never asked you for anything, but I'm asking you now. Help me. Help me find her and show her how much she means to me. Tell me what I can do."

"Well," Reagan said, her eyes sparking, and Nick feared he was in trouble asking the bad Stark sister for help. "There is one thing." Reagan went around the island in the kitchen and thumbed through a stack of papers and mail sitting there. She found whatever she was looking for and passed it to Nick. "She wants this house."

He peered down at the printout. It was a ranch-style white house with black shutters and a red door, a white fence surrounding it. The landscaping was immaculate, everything about the house charming. Never had Nick seen a house that looked more like Becca than this one.

"But you said she's moving right now."

"She is. Into an apartment. She couldn't afford the house; the bank denied her despite her having thirty percent to put down because she didn't have 'dependable employment.'"

"But what about the diner?"

"She quit to move to Lexington."

Nick eyed the printout again. "And you want me to . . . ?"

Reagan smirked. "They call it a grand gesture for a reason."

Chapter Eighteen

Becca dropped her last box onto the floor in the tiny open-floor-plan apartment and glanced around.

There was a kitchen. There was a family room. But it all sort of blended together, and the size of the space would easily fit into just her family room back home. Actually, the size of the entire apartment might fit inside her family room. The only bedroom was the size of a walk-in closet, and the only bathroom was barely large enough to bathe in. Two people couldn't stand inside it comfortably, so it was probably good that Becca would be living there alone.

She was alone. The word settled over her, and she thought it was time she got used to the idea of eating by herself at restaurants and having cats. Single people had lots of cats, right? Only Becca hated cats.

With a long sigh and a swipe across her forehead to catch a bead of sweat, she sat down on the floor because she'd decided not to bring any of her furniture with her.

Apparently, college towns had rental companies that would furnish a place, and then, when you moved out, they'd come pick it all up. And that sounded like music to Becca's ears until the rental company called to tell her they would be delivering her stuff a week late.

She thought longingly of the white house she'd found, how easy it would be for her to afford it with her new job at the Kentucky Tavern, a local steak house that was supposedly so packed the waitresses made a killing in tips alone.

But neither that, nor the 30 percent she'd agreed to put down, was enough for the bank to finance her. She'd considered listing the diner as her current employment, sure Sage would cover for her, but she was never the liar her sister was, and so she'd nodded okay and immediately sought out other options. Which was what led her to the apartment.

And really, the place wasn't so bad. Small, sure, but bad? Not really. It was within walking distance of campus and her job. She would save a ton on gas and her utilities were all included. Win-win.

But still, she hated the idea of not having a true home, which was why she'd elected to keep her grandmother's house back in Triple Run. As long as it was there, she would always have a place to go. Even if the thought of going back to Triple Run made her want to cry her eyes out.

With a long sigh for what might have been, Becca pushed off the floor and opened the door, prepared to head down for the last box, but instead she stopped short, narrowly colliding with the person who was on the other side of the door. The one person who could put her back together or wreck her completely.

She tried not to sigh with relief as she took him in, all faded jeans and Hamilton Stables T-shirt, his hair longer than usual, his glasses smudged on the right side from him adjusting them. "Nick? What are you doing here?"

Nick held up the box in his hands. "I was driving by and saw this random box out in a truck downstairs. Thought I'd bring it on up." At her pointed stare, he added, "And then I was hoping you'd come somewhere with me."

She peered around him.

"It's just me."

"How did you know where to find me?" she asked, then it hit her. "Ah, Reagan."

Nick nodded. "I was very convincing."

"I wouldn't give yourself that much credit. This is Reagan we're talking about." She crossed her arms and studied him. On closer inspection, he didn't look so good. The areas around his eyes were black, his hair a disheveled mess, and there were far more smudges on his glasses than usual.

"I just need a little bit of your time. I know I don't deserve it, but you were always the better person here. I'm hoping the good Becca will give the bad Nick a few minutes. A half hour max."

With a shake of her head, Becca's gaze found the floor. "I don't think that's a good idea. My heart . . . it's . . . I just don't think so. But thanks for the box."

"Becca, please. Just a half hour."

It hurt Becca to see him, but the temptation was still there. They'd known each other a long time, and she hated to throw away all that history. Still . . . she was moving forward and Nick was part of her past. "I don't think twenty-four hours of talking would change our situation. We want different things."

Nick cocked his head, and Becca fought the urge to go to him. Even angry with him, she struggled to resist him. "Then it's a good thing I don't want to talk. I want to show you something."

Curiosity moved through her. It was one of the few attributes she'd inherited from her grandmother, and Nick knew she struggled to say no when there was a mystery involved.

"Show me something?"

"Just show you something. I won't talk at all if you don't want me to."

Becca's gaze met his and her stomach tightened. God, did she ever love him. He was difficult and he'd hurt her worse than anyone else had dared, but she still loved him. "That's not what I want." Her heart throbbed painfully in her chest and she wished she could ask him to leave, wished he hadn't come at all. Yet she couldn't deny how good it felt to see him, how much she wished she could just put it all aside and go to him.

"Thirty minutes?"

A smile played on his lips, and Becca pointed at him. "This doesn't mean a thing. I'm just curious."

"Of course," he said knowingly.

"I hate that you know me so well."

Nick nodded, slower this time. "I'm sorry."

"Don't be sorry. Not for that. Not for any of it, actually. You shouldn't be sorry for how you feel just because I was hurt in the process."

He opened his mouth to respond, but Becca threw up her hand. "I can't do this. If we're going, let's go. But I don't want to talk about this."

Nick cleared his throat and took a step back. "Okay. No talking. I'll drive."

"Fine."

They settled into Nick's car, and Becca drew in the smell before she could order her nose to be good. Fresh linens and soap and just a hint of spicy cologne. It was so Nick, and instantly she remembered that smell overwhelming her as he hovered over her, his eyes on hers as they moved together.

God, what was she thinking agreeing to this? Her heart had just begun to cope and now she'd thrown it back into the fight, no warning and no hope of protecting it.

"Are you cold or too hot? Maybe too hot." Nick hit the A/C and cold air blew into the small space. Becca shivered and he hit the Off button. "Sorry, you're normally . . ."

"I know. And it's fine."

Their eyes met at a traffic light, and Becca felt her throat closing up, but then the light turned and they continued on to wherever they were going.

Nick tapped the steering wheel nervously as he drove, and Becca was wondering what all of this was about when she started recognizing things. The gas station on the last street, the CVS on the corner.

After another familiar turn, Becca sat up taller. "Where are we going?"

"You'll see."

"I know this street."

Nick swallowed. "I know."

Nick spotted his destination and pulled into the driveway, his heart beating so rapidly it might give out at any second, but he couldn't freak out. Not now. He'd worked through all the things he'd say, all the small, sweet things he felt might convince Becca that he cared for her and only her. But as his gaze landed on hers, eyes wide in question at him, only one thing came out.

"I love you. I know I should have told you that a long time ago, but there it is. And I had this list of things I wanted to say to you, but now you're looking at me, and you're so damn beautiful, and you're finally fulfilling your dream, and all I can think is 'damn, I love her so much.' I love you, Becca. And I've screwed up. A thousand times, probably, since I met you, but the biggest screwup of all was allowing you to walk away when what I should have done was beg you to stay. Ego aside, beg on my hands and knees. Because see, we're going to have issues. We're going to fight, and I'm going to be difficult sometimes and stupid even more often. But I want you, and only you. For the rest of my life." He waved a hand at the house. "Here, if you'd like. Or even if not, even if you say no and tell me to leave. This is yours. And not because I'm trying to buy your love, though I would if I thought that would work, but because you've been my best friend for all my life and I love you. I want you to be happy . . . even if it isn't with me."

Becca's eyes turned glassy and she peered back at the white house, the picket fence, then again at Nick. "So, what you're saying is that this . . . you . . . you bought me the white house?" Tears brimmed in her eyes, one breaking free in a slow trail down her face.

Nick reached out and gently swiped the tear away. "I bought *us* a house. If you'll have me. I know you think I'll never love you like I loved Britt, but that's where you're wrong. I loved you long before I met Britt. And while I'll always respect and remember her for the wonderful woman she was, Britt never had my heart. I gave it away the moment I met you. I realized that I was holding on to the past for fear that I would continue to experience the pain there, but that isn't the way to live. And I'm ready to live now. With you. I signed over my share of Industries. I've fixed things with my brothers and now, if you'll let me, I want to fix them with you. And maybe you'll never forgive me, maybe—"

"Shut up."

Nick pulled back. "Becca, please, I—"

Becca unbuckled her seat belt and climbed over the armrest until she was sitting in his lap. "You had me at 'I love you,'" she said, changing up the line from *Jerry Maguire*, a movie they'd watched together a thousand times. And then she leaned in and Nick's hands cradled her face, his mouth on hers, tears soaking their faces, but he didn't care.

For once, he knew what he wanted out of his life and she was right in his arms.

Epilogue

The time was ticking by too slowly and Becca thought she might go crazy any second. For some reason, when she'd pictured this day, she'd envisioned it at the beach, overlooking the waves. But instead it had become "an affair to remember." Or that was what the invite in the *Tribune* had said.

"Look who's in love."

Becca turned around in search of the familiar voice and grinned wide when she found Priscilla in Room 1, beaming despite the cast around her left arm. "What, did you get in a fight with Caroline over the mayor?" Becca joked.

Priscilla scoffed. "Like that would be a competition."

"True enough." Becca reached for Priscilla's chart, read through the specifics, and then tsked at the patient. "Fell climbing a tree? What in the world were you doing in a tree? You're in your sixties; you realize that, right?"

"Says my birth certificate, not my mind. And Curly Tom crawled up the tree. What was I supposed to do? Let my cat fall to his death?"

Becca thought *better the cat than you* but knew better than to say it. "Cats are built for that kind of climbing, and he would have survived the fall just fine. Haven't you ever heard that cats land on their feet? Priscillas? Not so much. You could have called the fire department or that mayor you're spending time with these days."

Priscilla grinned again. "I let him know when I need him, don't you worry." Then she took in Becca's name tag and the grin spread to take over her face. "I always knew you would do it, ya know?"

With Becca's emotions already so high, she had to look away, blink back the tears that threatened to pour down. When had she become such a crier? She needed to fix that, stat, or else she was going to lose all respect in the ER. "I know you did. Thank you for that. For everything. But now, if you're good, I need to head out. They tell me I have someplace to be."

"Becca . . . what time is it?"

Becca shrugged innocently. "I don't know, four?"

"You're getting married in an hour. One hour. And you're here working? Your mother would have your hide if she knew it. You've got makeup and hair and all that other mess to do. Pictures! Your photographer is probably beside himself."

"Something tells me they'll wait for me. I'm the bride, after all. Surely that means something, right?" She winked at Priscilla, but all joking aside, it was possible her mother was indeed freaking out and driving everyone else up the wall trying to figure out where Becca was and why she hadn't made it to the church yet. And it wasn't that Becca was trying to avoid getting married; she just wanted to avoid the whole giant wedding thing.

Who knew a town of so few could put together a wedding of so many? At last count there were supposed to be 500 people there, and that was 499 more than Becca cared about. All right, so maybe her parents. And her niece and nephew. But the rest? She could take them or leave them. The same with the fancy dress and crazy makeup and hair that she would never be able to brush out. The whole thing oozed a lifestyle that wasn't her.

But then she thought of Nick again, of the proposal in Fiji after one of their dives, the assurance that he would love her forever. She wished she could have frozen the moment and lived in it forever, happiness surrounding her. They should have gotten married there in Fiji, without all the hoopla of the event that was the Stark-Hamilton wedding. With the board of trustees involved and the invite in the paper, it had turned into a giant affair, and Becca had never been one to enjoy this much attention.

Sure she couldn't avoid it any longer, Becca said good-bye to the rest of the staff and walked out of Triple Run Memorial, a new skip in her step. She had completed her degree, was officially a nurse, and was well on her way to finishing her physician's assistant certification. Everything was wonderful in her life, happiness overflowing. Until she reached her Highlander and found her mother's car parked beside it, said mother seething as she stepped outside the car and marched toward her.

"Now, Becca Reed Stark, I know you're a mess of stubbornness, but this is too much. The whole town's expecting you to show and you do this? What will Nick think? He must be beside himself."

"Mama, I still have an hour."

"Are you insane? Your wedding started..." She checked her watch. "Six minutes ago."

"No, no, no. My watch clearly reads six after four, not five."

With a loud and dramatic sigh, her mother grabbed her arm and directed her toward the car. "You didn't set your watch after the time change last night, did you?"

Time change? "Oh my God. Oh my God! I'm late for my own wedding."

Her mother waved through the air. "I think I already said that. I'll text them that we're on our way."

"But there's no time for the dress and makeup and I look crazy. I can't get married in scrubs. Oh my God."

"Deep breath, baby girl. We'll get you there."

And she wasn't lying. They sped out of the hospital parking lot, ran two traffic lights, and Becca thought she might not survive this trip, let alone make it to the wedding. The tires screeched as her mother threw the car into park.

"Let's go, let's go."

Becca jumped out of the car and raced toward the door of the church, ignoring the crowd around the doors, the whispers that once again a Stark had pulled a Stark.

The main doors to the congregation were open, and she peered down the aisle, planning to just glance at it, take in the decorations, but then her eyes found Nick, in his beautiful suit, looking like he'd stepped out of a magazine. His eyes lifted and a smile as big as the sun spread across his face.

"There you are," he shouted. "Way to worry a man. Get on down here."

Becca's cheeks burned as all five hundred people in the congregation turned to look at her.

She held up a finger. "I'll be right back. Five seconds. I need my dress and makeup and..." Her eyes found Nick's again, and he started for her slowly, his gaze never leaving hers.

He reached out to her once they were face-to-face, his fingers threading through hers. "I don't care about the dress or the makeup or any of the rest of that. I only care about you, and to me, this is you."

"I'm in scrubs."

Nick shrugged. "Details. I never much liked those giant dresses anyway."

Becca laughed at the glare he would surely receive if her mother heard him say that. "I love you." Becca reached up to kiss him, and he held her close.

"So much," he said back. "Please marry me and put me out of my misery. Every second I wait to call you my wife is a second too long."

A loud huff sounded from behind them, and Becca's mother pushed her father at them. "She's at least walking down the aisle."

Nick grinned. "Fine. I'll just go back to my post. See you in a second, Becca Stark."

Becca's heart filled with warmth and she thought yes, this, this was the moment she'd waited for her entire life.

She walked back out with her parents and the ushers closed the doors to the congregation.

"He's a keeper, you know," her mother said, dabbing her eyes with a tissue. "Not every man would agree to marry you looking like that."

Becca rolled her eyes. "Thanks, Mama."

And then the string quartet someone had hired for the event— Becca had no idea who—started playing, and Becca expected to hear the wedding processional. Instead they played "Bless the Broken Road" by Rascal Flatts, and there was no holding back her emotions.

The ushers opened the doors and everyone stood, but Becca's eyes were locked on one person, the boy she'd fallen in love with all those years ago, now the man who would forever hold her heart.

Nick mouthed the words to the song he'd sung in her ear the night he proposed, dancing under a star-filled sky, unwilling to let go long after the band stopped playing and the crowd had dispersed. Because one thing Becca knew for sure: they had both traveled down broken roads, but those roads only ever had one end.

"I love you," Becca said as she reached him. "I will forever love you."

"I love you, Becca Hamilton." And then, ignoring the rules, the crowd, the head shakes of disapproval, Nick pulled her to him and kissed his best friend, his love—his wife.

About the Author

Melissa West writes heartfelt Southern romance and teen sci-fi romance, all with lots of kissing. Because who doesn't like kissing? She lives outside of Atlanta, GA, with her husband and two daughters, and spends most of her time writing, reading, or fueling her coffee addiction.

Connect with Melissa at www.melissawestauthor.com or on Twitter @MB_West.